A GOOD DAY TO DIE

Duncan Pryde Series

JAN DOMAGALA

Prologue

Haltor 2297ce

Wind rushed past him as he fell. The orbital jump was one of the most dangerous free fall jumps anyone could perform, as so many things could go wrong.

His suit covered his body, covering his fluid body armour underneath. The helmet on his head was light with a visor that acted as a Heads-Up Display.

Terminal velocity was reached quickly as he configured his body, arms tight against his sides and feet together as he pointed himself toward the ground. Opening his arms and legs wide gave him more control over his descent.

He waited until the last possible moment before reaching for the button on his flight suit that would deploy his parachute. The sudden drag from the air trapped in the chute as it opened out was jarring and, in many cases, had caused injury, snapping the head back against tanks held on the back.

The ground came rushing toward him, and he prepared for the landing. Taking the impact, he allowed his knees to bend sideways, keeping his legs together. He rolled onto the ground, coming up on his knees and releasing the chute in one swift fluid movement.

He was down and safe.

His landing spot was on the roof of a building at the base of a huge cliff. The entire structure was nestled tight against the cliff, giving it a secure, easily defendable position against infiltration. The cliff it nestled against was over three thousand metres high, a vertical wall that was too high to rappel down and too sheer to climb.

No one was thought to be insane enough to attempt a free fall parachute descent as the wind currents would bash anyone stupid enough to try it against the cliff wall. It would be suicide, even to think of it.

Duncan Pryde was that person.

He was an operative of the Ministry of Intelligence section Seven, designated Security Operations, or SecOps. They handled situations that ordinary people didn't want to dirty their hands with.

Intel had reached MI7 that a bioweapons facility was on this planet at this location. Duncan was tasked with infiltrating it, ascertaining if the intel was solid, and then closing it down permanently.

As soon as he was down, he released his harness, and the chute self-destructed. It had been coated with a chemical that, once activated, would flare up and incinerate the fabric in seconds, leaving no trace.

Taking out a small device no larger than a mobile phone, he used it to hack the locking control of the hatch on the roof. He replaced his Personal Information Network, or PIN, back in the pouch on his belt, then took out his SAP10 sidearm from his holster strapped to his chest. Racking the slide, he was ready to rock and roll. The pistol was already fitted with a small suppressor to minimise any sound of the gun being fired.

Lifting the hatch up on its sturdy metal hinges, he felt the recycled air escape from below, hitting him in the face. It was warmer than out here and smelled clean. It was possible that all the air was processed through filters to prevent any microbes or germs from travelling through the facility. This supported the intel that it was a bio-chemical weapons facility, at least partly. Many installations had clean air functions, especially if they were handling delicate computer systems, so this wasn't conclusive. Further investigation was required, obviously.

Dropping down through the hatch, he landed in a small room around twenty metres square. A door faced him, which led to the rest of this facility. Everywhere was white—white walls, white ceilings, and even a white floor—giving the impression of pristine cleanliness. Strip lights across the ceiling illuminated everything in dazzling detail.

Dressed as he was in his combat suit, which was all black, he was going to stand out like a sunflower in a poppy field.

A quick glance around showed him what he needed. There was a row of white coveralls hanging against the wall. He let his helmet recede into the recess in the collar of his suit, then picked a coverall that would fit and put it on.

He hoped it would suffice long enough for him to gain the intel needed to either confirm or refute the intel that had been the impetus for this mission.

Keeping his pistol hidden in a pocket, he cracked open the door to glance out through the slit. Everything seemed okay, so he opened the door enough to exit the room.

He stepped out onto a walkway that had a metal railing at the edge. The walkway overlooked a vast, cavernous room that was divided into several smaller sections, each with a transparent ceiling. This was so anyone up here could view each of the smaller sections.

Each section seemed to be a lab of some kind, which all had the containment levels of a biohazard lab. Each of them had an airlock leading to them, which they would decontaminate before leaving or entering to ensure the room was kept clean, and they took nothing out with them. Seeing this, his attention was quickly drawn to what was being done in them.

Others walked past him, ignoring him as they went about their duties. They were as oblivious to him as he was to them. He was focused entirely on those rooms down below and what they were doing.

He was no biochemist, so he had no real idea what they were working on. Taking out his PIN, he secretly took a video of the chamber below showing the different sectors, stopping long enough on each so the real experts could tell what they were actually doing. Once he had the footage, he transferred it through an encrypted burst transmission to his ship in orbit, which would then route it to MI7 HQ on Terra II. The whole process would take seconds as the relays were in place in Hyperspace for transmissions such as these. This was how interstellar communication was accomplished.

All he had to do now was wait for the verdict.

An alarm sounding throughout the facility told him he had no time to waste. The transmission had been detected, not the content or who it was sent to, just that an unauthorised transmission had been sent.

Duncan chided himself for not expecting this and failing to prepare for it. Now, his time had run out; he doubted his hastily prepared costume would mask the fact he was an intruder for long.

"That's him there," a voice shouted along the walkway, telling him he was right. He hoped his subterfuge would last a little longer, but things invariably never went as you expected.

People appeared behind him and from each side, cutting off any hope of escape in those directions. Hemmed in on all sides except one, he knew what he had to do.

A quick look around and over the railing told him all he needed to know.

Leaping over the barrier, he swung over it and under the floor he was on. Beneath this walkway was another level with the same sort of railing. His legs swung over this as he released his grip on the bar above and landed safely. He got to his feet and ran along this level as fast as he could, looking for a way out.

Bullets pinged off the wall as someone opened fire on him from behind. A quick glance over his shoulder told him where the shooter was. Pistol in hand, he returned fire in one swift, smooth move, dropping the shooter with a bullet to the chest.

Either these guys really didn't want anyone stealing their secrets, or this actually was a bioweapons facility.

The end of the walkway was approaching, and he had nowhere else to go. He knew there was another level beneath him, so he used the same manoeuvre as last time and swung over the railing to swing down onto it.

There seemed to be more guards about than he'd expected. This raised another question: had they known he was coming, and if so, how?

He'd had experience with bioweapons recently, which was why he had been sent to see if this was connected to the other incident. From what he was seeing, they weren't related, and he may not have been a biochemist, but he'd seen enough labs to know that whatever was happening here was not good.

Hoping his transmission had gotten through, he had little time to wait for an answer. His priority now was survival.

Another guard appeared at the other end of the walkway and fired a rifle burst. Duncan threw himself over the railing with little regard for what was below.

He was relying on his memory of the first time he'd glanced over the top railing and seen three layers beneath his. Swinging around, he landed on the last level, right in the middle of another group of guards.

How many were there, and had they waited for him on every level?

They all fell to the ground as he landed on them. Duncan was first to regain his feet. Seeing all the weaponry and the sheer number of guards he was facing, he knew there was no chance of fighting them all off. He did the only thing left to him and went over the railing once more.

He landed on the top of one of the labs he'd been watching. Lucky for him, the material it was constructed of was strong enough to withstand the impact of a grown man landing on it.

Not bothering to consider how lucky he was, he leapt to the ground from the roof. He quickly accessed his comms by touching his earbud, which was linked to his PIN, and called his ship in orbit.

"Ship, I need exfil immediately, and I also need an escape route from inside this place," he said.

"Copy that, Commander. Stand by; you will have an exit shortly," the AI controlling his ship replied.

Duncan looked around as more guards approached from both sides of the narrow walkway between the labs he was in.

"Ship, you'd better hurry. Time down here is running out," he said.

"I have you on the ground floor, Commander. I will make an exit for you in the south wall to your right in thirty seconds. I suggest you make your way over there as soon as possible, but do not get too close," the AI replied.

Duncan saw another gap through the labs to his right and ran toward it. Bullets followed his every step as the guards attempted to stop him.

Bits of flooring were thrown into the air from the bullets striking the ground as he ran. He heard the smacking sound as more shells hit the walls of the labs, and he hoped they were strong enough to withstand such a pounding. The last thing he wanted was for some deadly bug to be released through a hole in any of the labs.

Counting down the seconds, he knew he had at least fifteen left before his ride arrived. With nowhere to go, he turned and aimed his pistol down the narrow ally he'd just run down. It was only wide enough to allow one at a time to follow, which made them easy pickings.

The first one dropped from a bullet to the chest, the second tripped over the fallen body, and Duncan shot the one behind him, dropping him on top of the second guard. He looked up from beneath his comrade lying on top, and Duncan shot him in the face before he had time to free his weapon.

Another one appeared and fired at Duncan, who dropped to one knee. The hastily fired bullets passed harmlessly overhead, giving Duncan time to shoot the shooter before he had time to readjust his aim.

Four down and the seconds were counting down.

As Duncan aimed at another guard, the wall behind him exploded inwardly, blasting huge chunks of masonry toward him.

The explosion's heat seared the very air as it travelled through the facility on the shockwave.

He staggered to his feet, his ears ringing from the blast. He ran for the opening, leaping over debris from the wall, and dived through.

The outside of the facility was open to a vast expanse of flatland. The building had been erected away from any city or small colony to minimise the effect should anything be released from the facility and to maximise security. Duncan saw his ship hovering a few metres off the ground, fifty-odd metres away.

Sprinting for it, he said, "Destroy that building, use incendiary missiles, and incinerate everything."

Missiles left the front tubes of the ship streaking over Duncan's head as they headed for the structure he had just escaped.

The first salvo exploded in a burst of fire and fury; flames burned throughout the building. Another salvo was fired, followed by another, adding to the cataclysmic conflagration. By the time he reached the ship, the building was engulfed in flames. No one could survive that fire, and neither could anything produced there.

Making his way to the bridge deck, he watched the result of the damage caused by the missiles for a second, then said, "Okay, Ship, our work here is done. Let's go home."

____

Chapter 1

____

Terra II

The new headquarters of MI7 was in New London, situated near a river that utilised it for the business it was using as a cover. Universal Travel was a travel company that supplied vacations for the wealthy.

The actual headquarters for MI7 was beneath UniTrav's building on the ground level.

Duncan returned there after his mission on Haltor to deliver his report to Director William Chambers, his boss and the head of the Ministry of Intelligence.

C was in his office waiting for him when Duncan arrived, and upon entering, he knew something was wrong just by looking at him. His typical stoicism was missing, replaced by a frown and a dark look in the eyes.

"What the hell were you thinking?" C said before Duncan could even utter a syllable in greeting.

"Excuse me, sir, what are you referring to?" he said calmly. He was still acting in mission mode, so his emotions were strictly controlled.

"I think you know what I mean," C said. "TransGen, the owner of that facility, logged a report that they were attacked and that an agent from a corrupt government destroyed their facility."

Duncan listened closely. This made no sense. They couldn't possibly know he had been an agent. However, as he looked back, he wondered why so many armed guards had arrived soon after he had gained entrance to the facility. At the time, he'd remarked that it seemed almost as if they had expected him.

"It is a mystery to be sure, sir," he replied, adding nothing further.

"Why didn't you wait for confirmation before blowing up the place?" C asked.

"I didn't have time, sir. As soon as the transmission was sent, an alarm was sounded, and guards came from everywhere, and they weren't even considering capturing me," he explained.

"How can you be so sure?"

"Because they opened fire the moment they saw me, sir. No warnings, no attempt to capture me, they just shot on sight, and they were shooting to kill."

"I see. Isn't that a little odd?"

"I thought so at the time, sir, now even more so. I firmly believe they knew I was coming or that someone was. What they didn't expect was who they got and the determination I had to stay alive."

"Well, I can understand that, all right, but in the meantime, they have launched a complaint that must be looked into. Of course, because you destroyed any evidence of what they were making there, we only have your word about what you saw. They already denied anything illegal was being done there."

"How far up is this going, sir?" Duncan asked.

"As high as the new President; apparently, they have friends in high places and are determined to see this through. In that regard, I suggest you keep your head down until we know more ,or it's blown over."

"If they've taken this as high as you say, then I can't see it blowing over any time soon. I must gather evidence to support my claim then, sir."

"I can't authorise that as well, you know."

"I wasn't asking permission, sir. I am doing what I can to support my claim and protect the reputation of this organisation."

"I'm saying it again, Pryde. I can't authorise what you intend to do, so I'm giving you two weeks of R and R to wait this thing through. Do I make myself clear, Agent?" C said with the slightest hint of a smile.

"Perfectly, sir. Two weeks," Duncan replied. He knew what C had done, given himself plausible deniability and Duncan the opportunity and time to do as he suggested.

As he turned, he said, "I'll see you in two weeks, sir."

"Have a good time, Pryde," C replied, returning to work.

Duncan left the office and was met by Stephanie Goodchild, C's aide. She knew more about the daily running of MI7 that it was often joked that if she ever left, C would never be able to manage on his own.

"That was quick. Was it as bad as everyone suspected?" she asked, smiling to see him.

"I've been given two weeks leave until things blow over," he replied. He didn't return her smile; he just looked at her. He knew she was a beautiful woman who was always pleased to see him, but he struggled to make the connection into friends. It was something to do with his control of his emotions. It had hardened him to social interaction, making it difficult for him to make friends or even speak with people outside of work.

"Where are you going? Somewhere nice, I presume?" she said.

"I haven't decided yet. There are some things I need to do first, though."

"Such as?"

He gave her a slight head tilt. Why did people do that? Why was it so important for them to know everything you did every minute of the day? He found this kind of intrusion exhausting.

"Personal stuff, you wouldn't be interested in any of it," he said instead of what he wanted to say.

"Okay, then, I guess we'll see you in two weeks. Keep your PIN active in case something happens, and we need to reach you," she said.

He nodded, then turned to walk off.

He didn't like lying to anyone, especially Goodchild. Despite her incessant need to inject herself into his life, on some level, he liked the interest.

He had to admit that he actually liked her, too.

Putting that aside for the time being, he concentrated, first and foremost, on clearing his name.

Chapter 2

Somewhere on Tau Ceti III

The hooded man entered the dimly lit room. Looking around, he saw the long table that members of this select organisation sat around during meetings. This time, though, he was the only other occupant.

Number One, the head of the organisation, sat in his usual seat at the head of the table, also wearing the obligatory mask.

"Do you know why you've been asked to attend today, Number Four?" the enigmatic leader asked, his voice altered by a tiny device placed against his throat. It was impossible to know who the voice belonged to or even the gender of the person.

Number Four stood at the far end of the room and paused before saying anything.

"I would presume you are eager to know what progress I have made in terminating the agent who destroyed our Dust facility," he said.

"I understand you sacrificed our bioweapons facility on Haltor. I hope it was worth it," Number One said, and the meaning was clear. This group did not take failure lightly.

"Sir, I admit we underestimated his skills. He is a formidable opponent, but I have taken steps to minimise the damage. Before the news was leaked, I moved all our experiments to another facility. All that was being manufactured at this site were pharmaceuticals for the medical industry. I have had a statement issued regarding the attack, putting the blame on a government agency with proof that the facility was doing nothing illegal. In this way, I hope to isolate the agent from his agency while we set another trap for him."

"And what makes you think you'll succeed this time?" Number One asked, their voice rising slightly. Even through the alteration to their voice, it was clear that they were becoming impatient for actual results.

"The Ministry has disavowed him; they cannot admit that one of their agents was involved. This will make him more vulnerable; he will have no resources to call upon for help. There will be no escape this time."

Although it was kept hidden, this brought a smile to Number One's face.

"Ensure you send someone to deliver the bill for his interference in our affairs, and Number Four, make him pay dearly. I want the full price paid; do I make myself clear?" they said.

"Perfectly, sir."

"Carry on. The next time you contact me, I expect it to be with proof that the agent is dead. Nothing else is acceptable," Number One said and then dismissed him with a wave of his hand.

Number Four knew what had to be done, and he knew he would pay the price if he failed. He knew exactly the right person to assign this task to.

He was already making a secure call as he left the meeting hall.

Kalisto

The sun was setting over the ocean; moonlight glistened over the slight waves as they lapped against the shore.

He sat on the veranda of his home, overlooking this spectacular sight.

Stars winked in the clear night sky as it darkened with the onset of night. With no light pollution, the stars were clearly visible.

On the glass-topped table to his side was a glass tumbler filled with an aged Scotch over large chunks of ice.

The man sitting in the wicker chair reacted with disdain when the call came through. He touched the earbud in his right ear and said, "This had better be important."

When he heard the altered voice in his ear, he stiffened.

"I have a job for you," it said.

"When and where?" he asked.

"I have sent the details to your PIN. I want the target found and eliminated," Number Four said.

"Is there a time frame here?"

"The sooner the better. Just get in touch the usual way when you have completed the task with proof."

"Copy that."

"And Razor," Number Four said, pausing.

"Yes?" Razor replied.

"You ever talk to me like that again, and they'll never find your body. Do I make myself clear?"

"Perfectly, sir."

The call ended, and Razor took a long sip of his drink. He hated being at the beck and call of this shadowy group, as he had no control over any of his jobs, but the pay was excellent. As with any well-paid job, some stipulations came with it, and this was no different. The security surrounding this group was military-grade, and they had a zero-tolerance protocol for any wrongdoing. So he knew well what the voice meant when it threatened him.

Replacing his tumbler on the table, he took out his PIN to review the mission details.

The rest he was looking forward to was now as far away as ever as he saw who the target was and where he was located.

Knowing he had to get onto this fast, he contacted someone he knew who was on the scene. He would subcontract it out to him for the preliminaries and then get there to finish off.

Terra II

Duncan went home to re-evaluate his position. Sitting desk, he connected to his computer through his PIN.

He searched for everything pertaining to the facility he was at recently. Everything that came up supported the claim by the parent company, and he began to wonder if the intel he had been given was accurate or had been doctored somehow. If that was the case, what was their motive? He still destroyed the place and everything they were working on, so it wasn't to protect themselves, unless. What if they wanted him to go there and destroy it? They could then claim what they have done, that a corrupt agency sent an operative to attack their plant. That didn't explain the extreme amount of force he met once the alarm sounded.

Perhaps there was another reason for all this, and it was almost crazy even to consider it, but what if the intel was leaked, hoping he would turn up so they could kill him?

That seemed the most plausible theory except for this small detail. How did they know about him, and how could they be sure he would be the one sent there?

All he had at the moment was questions and no answers. If the latter supposition was correct, then for whoever this was to know about him, they had to have either a leak in the Ministry or had learned of him through an operation he was on.

That brought up more questions. If they had a leak, who could it possibly be? And furthermore, how would they be able to recruit from an organisation that no one was supposed to know about? If this were true, then whoever this was had some serious clout and would prove almost impossible to find.

His head throbbed from all the searching online and positing new theories, so he decided to take a break and get some fresh air. There was a park near his apartment that had a lake. He often took a stroll around it when he felt stressed, which, considering he had total control over his emotions, was a bit of a paradox. The truth was, he could control them for any length of time, but when he let down that impenetrable barrier, he felt drained from the amount of energy it took to maintain that level of control. He quite often had severe headaches from it and would need to unwind. Sometimes, he climbed; other times, he just went for a walk around the lake. He instinctively knew which would work, and this time, a stroll was what he needed.

The fresh air hit him like a jolt of coffee first thing in the morning. Breathing deeply, he felt the clean, crisp air start to work its magic, rejuvenating him already. Looking around, taking in the lay of the land, he set off for the park.

Chapter 3

"I have the target in sight. Follow him and see where he goes," said Marvin Gates, who was in charge of this operation. Razor had contacted him to use his team to keep watch on the target and relay details to him, the idea being they would learn what they could then draw up a plan for the hit.

Gates had other ideas. He was going to perform the hit to prove to Razor he and his team had merit. He knew that Razor had lucrative contacts that he hoped would include them for future work.

He sat in a van on the street where the target lived. They had positioned themselves there after the tracker placed on the ship he used had led them there.

This was the first time he had ventured out since returning home from the travel business he worked at.

He had positioned the rest of his team around the street so they could pick him up in whichever direction he took.

"I have him entering the park," one of his team reported.

Gates saw an opportunity. "Okay, close in. We'll do this here and now," he said.

Duncan spotted the tail as soon as he set foot out of the door. He had no idea who they were or who sent them, but he knew a hit team when he saw one.

He kept his gait relaxed, not indicating if he was aware of their presence. Wanting to draw them in, he headed for the park. Activating a secure comm channel through his PIN, he called Goodchild at HQ.

"Is there a watch order out on me at all?" he asked, keeping his voice calm and low so he wouldn't be overheard.

"No, Duncan, why do you ask?" she replied, immediately going to his tracker to check his location.

"Because I just picked up a tail, and I wanted to make sure it wasn't any of our guys before I hurt them," he told her.

"I have your location now, and I've informed C, and a backup team is on its way to you right now. Get to someplace safe and wait for their arrival," she said.

"Where's the fun in that?"

"Duncan, you don't have fun. What's going on?" she asked. She knew that he was all business, showing no emotion when on a mission, and from his voice, she knew that was his condition right now.

"True, but it's logical to try and find out who these guys are and who sent them. This is all too convenient after what happened with the last op for it not to be connected. Someone is out to get me, and I need to know who and why, or else my career as a covert operator is finished," he told her.

"Okay, I see it's no use trying to dissuade you from this, so just be safe. The backup team will be with you in less than five minutes."

"I'll either have my answers or be dead by then."

He finished the call with a touch to his earbud and concentrated on what was about to happen. He needed to stay focused. He entered the park, following the path past the open spaces where grass lawns with flowers edging them were a calming greeting. The path wound its way through several of these areas and onto a tree-lined pathway that led into a further space where climbing frames and other devices were set out for young children to play on.

Behind him walked a lone figure who he knew would not be alone. His teammates would be positioning themselves near the other entrances to cut off any chance of him escaping.

At this time of night, families had vacated the park, so there was little chance of bumping into any bystanders other than a few couples out for a late walk before retiring for the night or going to eat at a nice restaurant nearby.

That worked in his favour as well as it did for them. They thought they had him trapped; in fact, he had them exactly where he wanted them.

Past the play area was the lake, where he liked to either take a stroll around or sometimes just sit and stare into the water. It felt calming to watch the wind move the surface into ripples that stretched across its expanse, almost like some imaginary beast was walking along the bottom of the lake.

Several benches were placed around the edge, and he chose one that afforded him a clear view of the entire lake area. Sitting down, he waited. He didn't have to wait long as he heard someone approach from behind.

Gates watched as his target strolled through the park and took a seat on a bench near the lake. He had no idea he was being watched.

"This guy is no threat," another of the team commented.

"Look at him; he has no idea we're even here," the last one added.

"Keep the comments down. We have him now; move in," Gates ordered them.

"You took your time," Duncan said, glancing over his shoulder. Four men dressed in dark suits were spaced evenly behind him.

He knew who was in command by the way he kept his expression as neutral as he could. He was surprised for sure, but he didn't show it half as much as the three guys with him. They almost dropped their pistols when he turned to look at them.

Getting to his feet and walking around the back of the bench, he saw glances passed around from the three other members of this team while the leader kept his focus firmly on him. He saw in how his eyes narrowed that he was looking at him with renewed respect.

"Who sent you?" Duncan asked, getting straight to the point.

"You don't ask the questions here, pal," one on his right replied.

Duncan looked at him. "And yet I am," he said. "Anyway, I was talking to the organ grinder over there, not the monkey," he added, slowly turning his head to look at the leader on his far left.

Shock widened his eyes further. 'How did he know that?' he must've been thinking, Duncan guessed.

"Judging by all the weapons on display, I'm guessing you're not here to question me," Duncan said. "You do realise there is a backup team on the way," he added.

All four of them glanced around on hearing this, allowing Duncan to act.

Drawing his SAP 10, he fired at the three others, dropping two of them before the rest knew what was happening. The third was just reacting when another bullet hit him in the chest, knocking him over. The last one turned to see the pistol aimed right at him unwaveringly.

It was a stand-off, one neither of them was going to win.

"This can go one of two ways," Duncan said, "either we both fire and we die, or you tell me who sent you and why. I'll make sure they know you co-operated, I promise," he finished.

"What about option three?" Gates said and pulled the trigger.

Duncan saw the slight movement of his hand, the tightening of the finger around the trigger, and knew what he planned. The instant he recognised the movement for what it was, he threw himself down and fired his own gun. The bullet fired from Gates' weapon passed harmlessly over him, but his own found a more rewarding target. It hit him centre mass, knocking him back off his feet. By the time Duncan reached him, he was dying.

"Option three was we both fire, you miss, but I don't," he said as he watched the life leave his eyes.

Figures all dressed in black carrying rifles ready to fire invaded the park from every angle, all converging on Duncan's position.

The backup team had arrived.

Chapter 4

E mil (Razor) Razacovic arrived on Terra II too late to help. By the time he reached the scene, all the bodies had been whisked away, and the scene had been cleaned.

There was nothing for him to learn from it except that they failed.

As he surveyed the location, he used his skills to hack into the CCTV cameras placed around. Using his PIN, he downloaded the recent footage and took a seat in the park area away from the lake, which had been cordoned off as a crime scene. As he began reviewing the footage, it became clear that this target was not the usual prey and would need careful consideration.

He contacted Number Four with an update.

"I just lost four men who thought they could handle one man on their own. This is no ordinary target. He has skills and training, which means the price just went up," he said when the call was answered.

"Four men, you say. When you say lost, does that mean they were apprehended or something else?" Four asked.

"It means he killed all four just before a tac-team arrived to clean up."

"Interesting," Four said, then continued, "Okay, a slight change of plan. I want you to keep him under surveillance for a day or two. Don't engage him, and don't let him spot you. I'll be in touch with further instructions. Is that clear?"

"Perfectly," Razor replied. He didn't like the implications of him not doing anything further. It could mean they were going to replace him or terminate him for failing. Either way, he felt a chill run through him at the prospect.

Getting to his feet, Razor left the park. If he were going to be here for a day or two, he'd better find somewhere to stay. He'd return later to set up his surveillance. He had a few people he could call who could help with that, but he thought it best not to mention what happened with the last team he told to keep an eye on the target. They might think twice before taking the gig.

Once the call ended, Number Four sat back in his comfortable chair, thinking.

He had attended meetings all day and was about to go to dinner at his favourite restaurant with his wife when the call came through on an encrypted channel. Recognising who the caller was, the voice alteration software attached to his PIN activated immediately, keeping his identity from the caller.

Thomas Solvig was a prominent figure in government, an aide to the Secretary of Defence, James Marshall. Both men were aware of the workings of the Ministry for Intelligence, but only in a broad sense. They knew what they did in the respect that they handled delicate situations but not the details, and they had no idea who the operatives were for obvious reasons.

Solvig had a feeling that an operative had been responsible for the destruction of the Dust manufacturing plant and, as Number Four, was tasked with learning their identity and terminating them. This was no easy task because of the tight security surrounding the identity of the same operatives. He also had to be extremely careful not to give away who his real employer was.

He'd learned the name of the agent through his access to the confidential records in the Ministry. It had been a risk but turned out to be worth it. In his capacity as Number Four, he'd told Number One he had received information from a source about what the agent's name was. He didn't want the leader of a dangerous organisation like the one he had gotten involved in to know his real identity. The consequences for failure were final, which he'd seen played out in front of his eyes.

While seeming to keep the agent's name a secret, he was actively manipulating Marshall to look into the action taken at Haltor. Hinting constantly that no one was above the law and that if this was a rogue organisation, they had to be brought to bear.

He needed to do something to draw him out, something that he could not ignore, and once he did that, he would be a clear target. As an idea began to form, his lips parted in a cruel smile.

Duncan was sitting in a holding cell in the HQ, waiting to be interviewed. He was confused as to why he was being held here and not shown straight in to see C, but he was willing to see what occurred. Maybe he would learn the answer to that one from the next person through the door.

The door opened silently, and C entered, flanked by two of the men who had brought him in, the backup team.

"What were you thinking?" C snapped as he waved the two men out of the room.

"I'm not sure I understand, sir," he replied, genuinely at a loss as to what he meant.

"I told you to take some time off. That didn't mean slaughtering four men in your local park."

"They came after me, sir. What was I supposed to do, let them kill me?"

"You could have at least let one of them live so we could question him."

"I'll consider that the next time I'm faced with four armed men who are about to kill me."

"Jokes now, is it? You think this is funny, do you?"

"Not in the slightest, sir. This, what's happening here, that's as funny as hell."

"I'd think twice before your next witticism, Agent."

"I'm off duty, remember? You sent me home. If I'm off the clock. I don't have to treat you with respect, especially seeing how you're treating me as a suspect."

"I could end your career right this minute. You do realise that, don't you?"

"Do it then, or let me get back to work."

"You just said you were off the clock."

"You know exactly what I mean. You sent me home as bait to draw someone out. Now you're just pissed off that we didn't manage to capture one of them. Let me get back out there, and I'll find whoever is behind this."

C stood there, his hands on his hips, staring at him. Duncan could see he was right about him being frustrated at the missed opportunity of capturing one of them. It never occurred to him that he might be angry at him because he put himself at risk and could have died.

"You do realise you'll be on your own out there. I might not be able to send anyone to help next time."

"I realise that, sir."

"Okay, you win. Get back out there and see what you can uncover, and be careful. I'm only going to say this once, and if you repeat it, I will deny it. You are a valuable asset to this organisation. You are one of the best operatives I have, and I would hate to have to replace you. So be careful. Is that clear?"

"Yes, sir," Duncan replied. While his emotions were under control, he felt no response to the kind words, but he realised how hard it must have been for C to say them.

Without another word, he got to his feet and left the cell. He was eager to get back to work, even though, as C had pointed out, he had killed the only lead they had. So it was a good thing he had taken photos of the four men before they had been taken away. Now, he had something to go on.

Chapter 5

Chambers watched Duncan leave and knew he would continue with his investigation. While the Ministry was under scrutiny, it couldn't be seen to be helping him, not overtly at least.

On his way back to his office, he was greeted by Goodchild.

"Really, sir, you had him in the cells?" she said.

"We'll continue this conversation in my office if you don't mind," he replied, and the look in his eyes told her to remain quiet.

"Certainly, sir. I'm sorry," she said.

Once the two of them were alone in his office, he activated a privacy shield so that nothing said inside could be recorded or overheard from outside. Goodchild's eyes widened when she saw him do this, and C noticed her concern.

"Don't worry, you're not in any trouble here. Duncan might be, though. That's why I want you to keep a track on him at all times. Officially, we are not to be seen helping him until this internal review is completed. Unofficially, I want to give him all the help he may need."

Goodchild smiled in relief, "Copy that, sir," she said.

"I want you to check into the identities of the four men who attacked him. I want to know all their affiliations and who they work for both now and in their past. If necessary, dig into everything about them and turn over every stone until you have everything there is to know about them. No doubt Duncan will do the same, but if he can't access our data banks, then he will fall short in his enquiries. Reach out to him to let him know you will help."

"I will, sir. Who else will be in on this?"

"Until this review is done, I can't trust anyone. They had information about Duncan, which led a team right to him. I want to know how that was possible, and until we learn that, I'm afraid it's just you and I," C replied. He saw Goodchild swallow as the enormity of what he was asking her to do suddenly hit her. He knew her well enough to know she wouldn't baulk at the thought of this task and was gratified to know his trust in her was well placed when she smiled and said, "Copy that, sir."

"Good, I'll handle the review board so that you can get on with this, and I suggest you get on it ASAP. Duncan will not sit around waiting for them to make another attempt on his life. He will go after them. Do what you need to do to give him all the help he needs."

"Yes, sir," she said, still smiling.

"Go on then, get moving," C said, trying to hide his own smile.

When he was alone, he sat at his desk thinking about this review board that was going to look into their activities. How did they connect the incident on Haltor with the Ministry, he wondered, especially with SecOps? There were only a handful of people who even knew about them, and yet they were being investigated. How was that even possible? How was it that any other intelligence agency around the Coalition, however minor, was not even considered, and yet this one was the one they went straight to?

It sounded almost as if they were being targeted, specifically Duncan. For them to be that specific, they had to be within the inner circle, meaning there was a leak somewhere. Someone inside his own organisation was feeding intel to the review board so that they could come right to the source.

Since the disbanding of the Coalition Intelligence Agency, the Ministry had absorbed not only their cases but some of their personnel, too. Could it be possible that one of the new recruits held a grudge and was feeding intel to their enemies? The CIA definitely had garnered trust from its operatives, and when they were found to be running an operation to discredit the Ministry, and people were killed because their focus was entirely on the wrong target, the president had to step in. He disbanded the entire organisation and tasked the Ministry to handle their cases, absorbing the organisation into the Ministry. To handle the extra workload, their budget had been increased, and certain key personnel were taken on from the CIA to help. Now, it could be another ploy by the then-president, who had instigated the operation originally to bring down the Ministry internally. Even though the late president was no longer with them, having been killed in an attack on the Council HQ, his plan seemed to be going ahead without him.

He would look into this, but he would have to tread carefully. He didn't want to show his hand this early in the game and give away that he may be onto them. No, he would bide his time and see what happened, but he also had an idea of how to flush out whoever this leak was.

Duncan returned home and set to work right away. He accessed the MI7 databanks, input the images of the four men he'd gathered at the scene, and hit facial recognition search. Within a few minutes, he had their names and details of their lives, including who they had worked for.

"There you are," he said as he read the files. "Now then, who sent you, I wonder?" Searching through their work history and known associates, he came across a name he recognised. Emile Razacovic was known to the security services around the Coalition. He was known as a fixer; if someone had a problem, he fixed it for them. This usually meant the problem would disappear.

The interesting thing was that Razor, as he was known, had just arrived on Terra II.

"Now," Duncan mused, "why would you suddenly turn up on my doorstep?"

Chapter 6

Solvig had spent most of the evening out to dinner with his wife. As soon as he got back home to his luxury apartment, he began work in his study on his new plan.

The next morning, he woke, took a shower, and dressed in a clean, dark blue suit. As he checked his appearance in the full-length mirror, he smiled at what he saw. In remarkably good shape for a man his age, he looked like a politician. His dark hair was turning grey at the temples, the only indication of his true age. His youthful face and easy smile put people at ease the moment they saw him. Using the PIN to connect to a secure comms network, he called Razor.

"I want you to take over a project we have already set up. When you are in place, contact me with an update. Everything you need to know is in the file," he said, then touched his ear bud to end the call.

Pleased that everything was going as planned, he left his bedroom and went down to breakfast with his wife.

Razor was drinking coffee at a local shop near to where his target lived. He reacted slightly when the call came in, looking around at the faces seated nearby to see if any of them were aware of what was happening right there in their midst. No one was watching, not even glancing his way, which he found slightly amusing. Ignoring them equally as they were him, he took out his PIN and began to review the file sent to him.

His smile broadened when he saw what it was. He quickly paid for his coffee through the chip implanted in his forearm, then left the shop.

He had work to do.

Duncan had worked through the night to find out who had employed Razor but had drawn a blank. He finally called it a night and went to sleep around three a.m.

He was still feeling the effects of not getting enough sleep when he woke up the next morning. His internal clock never let him sleep past six a.m., so he climbed out of bed, went into his bathroom, and showered. As the hot water eased away his tensions, he came alive a little more.

Once he was finished, he got dressed in something more casual than his usual suit. A tee shirt and cargo pants would suffice for the time being. He was off the clock, after all.

He may be off the clock, but he was still connected to the system, so when the call came through, he wasn't at all surprised.

"Good morning, Goodchild. Aren't you supposed to be at work?" he said.

"I am, and I'm acting under orders from C himself. I looked into the men you killed in the park and found out something," Goodchild said.

"Same here. I'm afraid I used our data banks last night to do some research. I found out who they were and who they worked for," he said.

"Razor? Yes, I found out he was on a flight that landed here yesterday," she told him. "But did you know that he is leaving here this morning? I learned he has a charter flight leaving in a few hours."

"No, I did not. Where is he heading?" Duncan asked.

"He's going to Remar IV," she told him.

"What is he going there for, I wonder?" he mused.

"That's something you'll have to figure out, Duncan. Now listen, C is working hard at keeping the review board contained, but he wants me to liaise with you strictly off the record. He seems to think we might have a mole who passed data about you to whoever is after you. He cannot be seen to be helping you. That's where I come in, so tell me what I can do to help," she said.

"Just be there if I need you, Steph. It's good to know I have someone watching my back," he said.

"I'll keep track of you, but if you get into trouble, there might not be much I can do to help, not until this review thing is done with, but I'll do what I can."

"Copy that," Duncan said, then ended the call. He was basically on his own in this.

He left his apartment, got into his car, and drove straight to the spaceport where his ship was berthed.

"Ship, prepare for take-off immediately," he said as he parked the Nimbus in the docking area of his ship.

"Commander, I have been informed of your off-duty status. Strictly speaking, sir, your access to official channels has been revoked," the AI replied through the comm link.

"I'm evoking Command Override Alpha," he said, but before he could finish, he was interrupted by the AI.

"There is no need, sir. I have been given permission to help in your operation," his ship said.

"Thanks," he replied. He was genuinely pleased that C had not abandoned him. Officially, he was not helping, but he had allowed others to do so, supposedly without his knowledge or consent, giving him plausible deniability, an asset every leader or politician needs in their armoury if they ever want to survive.

Duncan went forward to the bridge and sat in the command chair as the engines came online and the ship lifted off the landing pad.

It took only a few minutes for them to exit the planet's atmosphere, and as soon as they were clear, the ship made the jump to hyperspace.

Chapter 7

While Duncan was pursuing his only lead, C was about to begin a meeting with the review board, chaired by the Secretary of Defence, James Marshall.

Marshall was a career politician, but he was a lazy one. He listened to his advisors and aides far too much, allowing them to do most of the work, which he then signed off on. This was probably the most work he had been forced to do personally for a long time.

He was wealthy, as most were in this line of work. The benefits of leadership were not just having the satisfaction of helping others, which had never concerned him, but the limitless opportunity to help one's self, to further one's career, and add to personal wealth. Those were the priorities foremost in his mind, nothing else. He even looked at this review board as an opportunity to score points with the new president and possibly add a few more lucrative contacts he could manipulate for further gain somewhere down the line.

Not knowing much about his job and this specific situation in particular, he relied heavily on his aide, Thomas Solvig, who sat at his elbow at the inaugural meeting of this board. For this meeting, the two of them were going to speak with the head of the Ministry of Intelligence to get a feel for what was to come.

The meeting was held at the temporary Council headquarters while new premises were being built. For this purpose, they had taken over the entire top five floors of the Imperial Hotel and increased the security in the building. Most of the usual hotel business had been suspended while the Council was in attendance until they could move into their new building.

C arrived early and was shown into the large conference hall, which he knew was to intimidate him. It was meant to convey that the Council had all the power, and he was alone.

He took a seat at the far end of the long table and sat with a calm expression on his face while he waited for the others to arrive.

Waiting for them, he kept an eye on the time. Ten minutes after the allotted time for the meeting, the two men entered and immediately took their seats at the opposite end of the table.

C had kept calm throughout his wait, his face neutral as he wondered what the game here was. He didn't have to wait for too long before they made their intentions obvious.

"What can you tell me about the incident on Haltor, Mister Chambers?" Marshall said, getting right to the point. It was obvious his intention was to throw C off guard with such a direct question, but C was having none of it.

He simply sat relaxed, looking directly at Marshall, and paused as if he was gathering his wits or calming himself down. Neither was the case here, though.

"Yes, I'm fine, thanks. No, it doesn't matter that you were late; I realise you're a busy man, too, and there's no need to apologise," he said.

Marshall looked at him with a half-smile before saying, "Excuse me."

"You're excused. Are we done here?" C replied.

Marshall was about to explode in anger. Instead, he said, "No, we are not done here; we haven't even begun yet."

"Then perhaps you should have arrived on time, and it's Director Chambers, not Mister."

"Oh, I get it. You thought I disrespected you. Well, that's just dandy. We have more important things to discuss other than whose dick is the biggest."

"You have that dubious honour," C said, repressing a satisfied smile.

"Thank you. Now, shall we proceed?" Marshall asked, and then the insult hit home, and he realised how stupid his gratitude made him look. When he looked at the man at the opposite end of the table, his eyes held nothing but contempt and fury. Chambers, on the other hand, had a stoic expression that hid his smile.

Clearing his throat, Marshall carried on.

"I'll ask again. What can you tell me about the incident on Haltor?"

"Nothing."

Confusion creased Marshall's forehead in a frown, "What's that supposed to mean?"

"Exactly what I said," C reiterated.

"You can't tell me anything because you don't know anything, or you can't tell me?" Marshall asked, desperate to get to the truth.

"Either one. It doesn't matter," C said.

"Why not?"

"Because I can't tell you."

"This is getting us nowhere."

"I could've told you that before we got here."

"Director Chambers, are you deliberately avoiding my question?"

"No, I answered your question."

"But you didn't, answer my question, I mean."

"You asked what I could tell you of the incident. I replied, nothing. That is an answer. Derive from that what you will."

"Okay, let's try this another way. It's my belief that an operative of an agency was involved in the said incident. Is that true or not?" Marshall questioned and smiled because, in his opinion, he had given Chambers no way out but to answer.

"I can neither confirm nor deny that."

"Excuse me, what?"

"Mister Marshall, is your hearing as defective as your intelligence is insufficient? I understand modern medical techniques can work miracles."

"Will you answer my question or not?" Marshall said, his voice rising almost to the point of a shout.

"I thought I already had."

"Director, I will get to the bottom of this, so if I were you, I would start thinking of cooperating with this board."

"This board? This is nothing more than an inconvenience. What I want to know is how someone gained access to top-secret information about my agency. I would like to know how that information was leaked to an outside source that has ties to a criminal organisation. These are the questions you should be concerning yourself with and not getting involved in some witch hunt."

"Careful, Director, your mask is slipping a little there," Solvig commented, adding his voice for the first time.

C looked across at him.

"There he is," he said, recognising where the power truly sat between these two.

Marshall looked at the two of them, completely oblivious as to what had transpired between them. Finally, he said, "I will take those comments under advisement, but for now, we must continue with this meeting."

C got to his feet, "I'm afraid we'll have to reschedule. I'm late for another meeting. Some of us have real jobs to go to," he said and walked toward the door.

"You can't just leave like that. I didn't give you permission," Marshall blustered.

"If you need me, you know where to find me, and if you don't know, ask your friend sitting next to you. He seems to know a whole lot more than you do."

With that, C left the room, leaving at least one of the men inside confused as hell as to what had just happened. He was certain Solvig knew exactly what went on, which gave him someone to focus his attention on.

Chapter 8

Remar IV

Razor sat in the comfortable seat in the passenger section of the starship, chartered especially for this trip.

He was able to view the planet below through a viewscreen on the hull near his seat as they entered the planet's atmosphere.

He knew his destination was somewhere in the outback, away from civilisation, but that's as far as it went. Everything else was a blank.

Their entry vector took them away from the cities where the colonists lived and straight toward the outback desert areas.

The ship slowed as it neared the ground, and he could see where they were headed more clearly.

There was a compound below that was fenced off as a security measure by a tall wire fence topped with razor wire. At each corner stood a guard tower watching over it and providing more security. As they got closer, he could see guards manning a pulse cannon inside each tower and more anti-aircraft pulse guns just inside the fence.

There was plenty of activity inside the massive compound as groups of recruits went about performing training tasks. He was impressed. He hadn't seen this level of intense training since he left the military. The compound was larger than three football fields placed end to end, and at the far end was an area where aircraft, including smaller starships, could land. It was clear that was where they were headed.

The landing was concluded with no concern of those training in the camp. Razor exited the ship to be greeted by a contingent of guards, all armed with sidearms and assault rifles.

"We've been expecting you. Follow me, and I'll show you to the commander's office," the leader of the small group said. They were all dressed similarly: black roll-neck shirts, black cargo pants, and boots. There were no signs of rank or authority on any of them, so he wondered how they knew who was in charge.

He gave a nod of acceptance and followed on after the leader as the rest of them either flanked him or carried on behind him. Either way, they made it almost impossible for him to make a run for it.

"What's with all the security?" he asked, indicating all the men around him.

"For your protection, sir," replied the leader as he was walking in front. This got Razor thinking. He wondered what exactly he was doing here; what did the mysterious voice on his comms want him to do? He thought he'd been employed to take care of that guy in New London, who was clearly more than was described. Was this connected to that operation, or was this something else? Was this the price of failure for not completing the hit? If so, they could have employed any number of assassins to terminate him, and he wouldn't have seen it coming. He knew because he'd done it more than once himself. If that was their purpose, why bring him all the way out here? It would make disposal of his remains that much easier, he supposed, but he was sure something else was going on, and as he saw an officer approaching, he knew he'd get his answers soon.

"Tell me again how we know he came here?" Duncan asked as they emerged from the hyperspace window back into normal space close to Remar IV.

"The target boarded a flight that had been chartered specifically to here, sir. Their flight plan was logged into Flight Control, and I have scanned the area and detected the energy signature from their engines to a place on the surface in the outback, sir," the AI replied.

"And you're certain it's them and not a similar starship? I mean, they could have changed their destination once the flight plan had been logged with Flight Control to throw us off the scent."

"That is possible, sir, except for the fact that each engine has a distinctive signature, rate of decay, the exact way the fuel is burned, and so on. Every engine, although built from the same design and using the same fuel, all are slightly different, which is how we can trace them through the signature, sir, as I'm certain you are aware," the AI said.

"I was just checking, Ship, just checking," Duncan said.

"If I may, sir, it's not like you to have doubts. Is there something wrong, sir?" the AI asked.

"There is something not quite right about any of this. Why is he all the way out there in the outback? There's literally nothing around for thousands of kilometres, which can only mean that the opposite is true. There is something out there, and it's hidden."

"Your hypothesis seems to be true, Commander. I have been scanning the area in which the energy signature travelled, and it supports your theory. There is a compound there, and the ship landed in the middle of it," the AI confirmed.

"Okay, Ship, take us down there, but let's keep off their sensors, just in case we're expected," Duncan suggested.

"Copy that, Commander. Taking us in," replied the AI.

The flight through the atmosphere was uneventful. The AI put the ship on a horizontal flight path a thousand klicks from the compound.

"Any signs of activity yet?" Duncan asked. He watched the forward viewscreen, which displayed the compound in high def. As far as he could tell, everything seemed to be normal. There seemed to be nothing happening that would indicate they were even aware they were here.

"Nothing so far, Commander," the ship replied.

"Keep a sensor lock on them. The moment something...."

"Incoming!" the AI warned, interrupting him.

Duncan saw the warning indicators all light up on the control panel in front of him. They had fired a brace of missiles at them, which had acquired a target lock as soon as they were airborne.

The AI immediately threw the ship into a vertical ascent and then into a series of twists and turns designed to throw off the sensor lock the missiles had on the craft.

This sudden series of evasive manoeuvres caught Duncan off guard. No human reflexes were a match for an AI, and he was thrown out of his chair. Landing hard on the deck, he scrambled to get back into the chair. The inertial dampeners had prevented him from being turned into strawberry jam against one of the bulkheads, but even so, he was bounced around pretty hard.

Regaining his seat, he was just in time for the inevitable.

"Brace for impact," the AI warned seconds before an explosion threw them into a tailspin, heading directly for the ground.

Chapter 9

"Did you get him?" Razor asked. He was in the command tent along with the leader of this group, Mikhail Polikov. He was an average-looking man with short dark hair and a face that had seen better days.

He turned his weathered features to him and said, "What did you expect?"

"I never expected it to be this easy, or why was I sent here?" Razor questioned.

"Oh, he's not dead, not yet at least. That's your job. We just delivered him to you, that's all. Your boss and ours wanted him here so we could find out more about him. He wants you to learn who he is and who he works for before you kill him. Like I said, we just delivered him to you," Polikov explained. He turned to the others in the tent with them, "Go and bring him here to our friend. We have a place already set up for you. Come, I'll show you," he said, looking once more at Razor.

They exited the main tent and went to the one a few metres away. Throwing the flap that formed the entrance to one side, they entered. It was dark inside, lit only by a few lamps, which added to the menace Razor felt as soon as he walked inside. There was a chair in the middle of the room fitted with straps on the armrests and the front two legs. Standing next to it was a table holding various tools of torture, as well as a selection of injector guns filled with coloured liquid, all designed to get at the truth out of the prisoner should the physical efforts fail.

"Very thorough," he said as he walked closer to inspect them. "All the toys a budding psychopath would ever want," he added with a sadistic smile.

"When he arrives, he'll be all yours. Learn as much as you can, then kill him. We'll dispose of the body later. I'm going to give a sit-rep to our boss. You wait here," Polikov said before walking off.

Razor watched him exit through the flap, leaving him with two of his men, both with the dead eyes of a killer. He wondered if the same fate awaited him that he was about to deal to his target.

As soon as he regained his seat, the AI instigated safety protocols, and a harness wrapped itself around Duncan, holding him firmly in place. The AI was running several scenarios through its quantum brain and considered all the possible outcomes for each one.

When the missile was going to hit, and the AI knew there was no way to avoid, evade, or prevent it, it did the only thing left that it could. It safeguarded the passenger.

A pod came up from beneath the command chair, cocooning it, and then the entire seat was dragged down into the section below the bridge and ejected through a hatch in the hull, propelling Duncan out and safely away from the explosion that destroyed the rear section of the ship.

As he was rocketed away from the ship, Duncan felt thrusters fire, which changed the trajectory of his pod. A quick burst was all that was needed to right his trajectory, sending it up into the air so the parachutes could deploy. From this position, he was able to watch his ship head down, out of control, in a desperate tailspin. Smoke billowed out from the rear section, the main engine gone, steering thrusters inoperative, leaving a dark trail through the sky until it hit the ground in one final explosion that threw flaming debris out over a vast area. From the size of the explosion, Duncan deduced that the AI had initiated the self-destruct protocol, timing it with its impact with the ground. In that way, it would look as if the ship was destroyed in the crash and not purposely so that none of the tech could be salvaged by the enemy.

As he floated down to the ground on the three parachutes that had deployed once he was ejected, Duncan knew he was really on his own now. All he had with him was what he was wearing and his sidearm. Luckily, he still had his PIN through which he would be able to contact HQ unless they were jamming comms.

A Mayday message would have been transmitted back to HQ the moment they were under attack, one of the many things the AI would have done as it reacted to the threat. It would have been a burst transmission straight through hyperspace relays on encrypted channels to ensure it reached the required destination. Whether or not they reacted to it would be another matter. He hoped Goodchild intercepted it before it went through official channels, which could mean it being ignored if the review was still underway.

A group of armed men were approaching his position in ground vehicles that looked like they could handle any terrain. All he could do now was wait until he landed. There was nothing he could do to prevent this. He just hoped they were a welcoming party and not a lynch mob. If these belonged to the same group who had fired the missiles at him, then there was little chance of them being the former.

His assumptions were confirmed as they formed a ring around his landing zone and aimed their assault rifles at him.

That could've gone better, he thought as his escape pod touched down in the middle of them.

One man came forward to open the pod door. He aimed his assault rifle at him, "Come out slowly with your hands where I can see them. Don't give my men any reason to fire. They haven't killed anyone today, and some have itchy trigger fingers," he said.

Duncan gave him a slight head tilt, "And you thought it wise to bring along unstable members of your team to bring me in?" he said.

The leader of the team stared at him. The sight of all the weapons aimed at him, plus what he'd just commanded, had been designed to intimidate him, but clearly, it didn't.

"Oh, you think you're a hard ass. I like that. Let's see how hard you are after we get through with you," he replied.

"Look, clearly there's been some sort of mistake here. I work for Universal Travel, and I was sent out here because we are looking into expanding the business. We had this idea that some clients might like the outback experience, you know, surviving out in the desert, in the wild. We'd send guides with them naturally; it would be bad for business if we killed off paying customers. Clearly, I've trespassed into an area we weren't aware of that was already occupied, so if you allow me to leave, then no harm, no foul, as they say. Of course, I'll have to arrange for someone to come pick me up, seeing as how you destroyed my ship, but I'm sure we can work something out over that," Duncan said.

The leader looked at him, saw his sidearm in a holster beneath his jacket, and held out his hand for it. "Do all representatives of your business carry weapons?" he asked as Duncan carefully placed his SAP 10 in his hand.

"It's a dangerous galaxy out here. It's best to be safe," Duncan replied.

He looked at the calm expression on Duncan's face, his eyes narrowing in suspicion. He glanced at his men, then turned his attention back to the man in front of him and said, "Come with us, and we'll get to the bottom of this. If what you say is the truth, then you have nothing to worry about." He let the implication of whether the reverse was true hang in the air between them.

Duncan went along but only because he couldn't see any other option, especially if he wanted to stick to his cover story. Live to fight another day was logical, so he hoped he would survive the next few hours so that he could take his chance when it arrived. The fact that he hadn't been killed on the spot proved that they had something planned for him. That gave him some leeway. He would have to see if it was enough for him to survive.

Chapter 10

MI7 HQ, Terra II

Goodchild was monitoring Duncan's vitals as he approached his destination and noticed a spike in his adrenaline. Although he could well manage his emotions, natural bodily functions were just that and something out of his control. He had learned to handle how he reacted to things such as a sudden adrenaline rush, along with fear and all the other emotional responses, so no one could tell, but his body reacted just like everyone else's.

After checking his location, she saw a notification of a burst transmission arriving. With all the data being compressed and encrypted, only the computer was capable of decoding and making it legible for human ears to hear. Directing the transmission to her location, she waited the few seconds it took for it to be unravelled. As soon as it was done, she selected open and listened to the transmission, her eyes widening the more she heard.

"Oh Christ, Duncan, what have you gotten yourself into?" she said. This was too important not to bring to C's attention, but he had given specific orders for her to manage things herself and not involve him. She was pondering the best way to proceed when C walked into her office.

"Is there any news from Duncan?" he asked.

"Sir, you told me not to inform you and to handle it myself."

"Never mind that. After my first meeting with the board, I have reason to suspect that the leak may be someone involved with the review and not within this organisation after all. I'm not ruling it out entirely. They had to have gotten certain details from within to be able to pass them on to those outside, so as long as we keep this to those we know we can trust, I feel we'll be okay to move forward."

"In that case, sir, I think you should hear this."

She played the transmission for him after activating a privacy shield around her office as a precaution and watched his expression. His lips pressed together as his brow furrowed.

"The bastards knew he was coming," he said.

"Seems that way, sir, yes," she agreed.

"We can't send in a tac team; it would give away our hand and inform them we are aware of their actions. Duncan is on his own, and I mean literally. There is nothing we can be seen doing to help him," C said as he turned his attention to his aide. He saw she was about to argue when he put up a hand to halt her.

"So, we have to ensure it appears as if we are doing nothing," he said, which brought a smile of understanding to her face.

"Where is Agent Sanchez at the moment? I understand she is due some R and R. Is that correct? Perhaps we could suggest some places she might want to visit on her time off," he said. When he was sure she understood, he nodded and left the office. "I'll be interested to hear if she liked where she went, you know, for future reference, should I decide to take a vacation myself," he added just before he left, closing the door behind him.

Getting to work immediately, she contacted Agent Veronica Sanchez.

Haltor

Sanchez, at that moment, was looking into the incident that Duncan had been accused of recently. She was acting on her own cognisance because she knew what Duncan was like, and he would never do the things he was accused of unless the intel was wrong.

The scene of the incident had been cleared; the facility had been destroyed and declared a crime scene. The initial investigation had either been extremely fast or not at all because there was no evidence anyone had ever been there.

Something didn't seem to sit right here, and she was now leaning toward the theory that it had been set as a trap to bring him out into the open.

From the scans she performed upon arrival, there was no trace of any chemicals, pathogens, or viruses ever having been there. Duncan would have had no need to run these scans as he had been working on intel that supported the claim that dangerous bio-weapons were not only being stored there but manufactured there, as well. Considering the recent case they had worked on together where the Omega Five virus had been discovered, it was obvious why this seemed to be in need of direct urgent action.

According to his report, Duncan stated that once he transmitted the video of the interior of the facility showing the different biohazard sections, he was attacked by men using lethal force to prevent him from leaving. He took that to mean the intel had been correct.

Everything pointed to his mission being a clean one, and he took the correct steps to conclude it.

So why were they claiming otherwise? Was it just to cover their backs or something else? If the intel was correct and it was a facility as was stated, then why claim otherwise? Surely they would simply cover their losses and move on. Criminal cartels rarely made a claim against the authorities for closing them down. On the other hand, legitimate businesses did.

She was pondering the details of this case when she was contacted through her PIN. Reaching up to touch her earbud, she activated the comm channel.

"Go for Sanchez," she said, then listened for a few seconds as Goodchild filled her in with the new details. When she was done, she said, "Copy that. I'm on my way."

Her ship was on the ground in front of the area where the facility had once stood in front of the cliff face. As she walked toward her, she said, "Ship, prepare for take-off. Set course for Remar IV. We're leaving as soon as I'm on board."

"Copy that, Agent Sanchez," her ship's AI replied.

As soon as she was on the bridge and seated in the command chair, the ship fired thrusters to take them up into the air.

"Course laid in, and the main engines are charged up. The jump to hyperspace is at your discretion, Agent Sanchez," the AI informed her. She watched the ground drop away as they rose high into the air. The sky darkened as they left the atmosphere, and the stars became more visible the higher they went.

She took a second or two to marvel at the sight of the vastness of space all around her, something she hoped she would never tire of seeing, before she said, "Okay, Ship, make the jump."

Chapter 11

Remar IV

Inside the tent, Duncan saw the seat in the middle, surrounded by all the instruments. He tried to remain calm as he knew what was coming, and despite being in control of his emotions, a chill still ran through him.

"So you claim to work for Universal Travel, is that right?" the leader of the compound said as he moved to the side. Another figure came from further inside the tent to stand next to the ominous chair.

"We'll soon see if that's the truth or not," he said.

"This is Razor. He'll be the one who will get to the bottom of this. I would advise you to tell the truth, but it doesn't matter really. If you are an operative, that suggestion would only fall on deaf ears. On the other hand, if you are innocent like you claim, then you will tell us everything we want to know anyway."

Duncan pretended to be scared now that he saw what was in store. He shook his head and turned to the leader, his face contorting with fear. Eyes wide, he said, "What're you going to do, torture me? There's no need. I already told you I work for UniTrav. We scout out possible places for vacations, some for the super-rich and others for ordinary people. I'm just doing my job here. If you let me go, I promise never to come back. I'll tell my boss that this place is unsuitable. We'll never come back again. What's more, we'll make sure no one does. You'll never be bothered again; I give you my word."

"As I said, we'll soon know if what you're telling us is the truth," the leader said, then waved his men forward to take him to the chair.

Duncan reacted fast. He struck the leader a blow to the throat and then pushed him into the men advancing on him. They all went sprawling onto the ground, and he turned to go in the opposite direction. He needed to get out of there and fast.

Another guard came at him, swinging the butt of an assault rifle at his face and hoping to take him down. He ducked, hit the man in the stomach, then grabbed the rifle and twisted it from his grip. Turning the rifle, he fired a three-shot burst into the man's chest, dropping him. Stepping over the body, he ran for another exit.

He found that the exit was also blocked by two burly men. One swung a blow at him, which he ducked, but the other hit him with a solid blow to the side of his head, knocking him to the ground.

Stars danced before his eyes for a second. As he tried to raise himself up, he saw three men standing over him, all pointing assault rifles at his face.

Another man came into view; Razor was his name. He smiled before saying, "Well, that clears that up. Why don't we find out what else you're not telling us, shall we?"

Before he could respond, another blow to the face knocked him back down to the ground. Pain exploded inside his head before darkness took the rest of his senses, and everything went quiet, then black.

"There you are," Razor said as his senses returned, along with intense pain. It felt like a horse was galloping inside his head, every pulse of pain in tune with the individual hoofbeats.

He tried to move but found he was firmly strapped to the chair he had seen earlier. The only thing he could move was his head.

"You've got the wrong man," Duncan said, his voice sounding harsh, even to him.

"Well, looking at the effort and skill you indicated in your attempt to escape, I think even you can admit that it disproves what you're trying to tell us. Don't worry, though; we'll soon get to the bottom of this," Razor replied with far too much confidence for Duncan's liking. He was acting like a man who knew that he had absolute control over the situation, and that bothered him. He hated not being in control of himself, and to be forced to relinquish that control to someone else was terrifying to him.

He had to remain in control of what he had left. He couldn't allow his captor to see that he was unsettled.

"You don't seem to understand. You have the wrong guy. I was just desperate to get away, as anyone would if they were faced with this. The skills you say I displayed, those are just what each member of UniTrav is forced to take—close-quarter combat, you know—in case we get into trouble. That's also why we carry sidearms, for protection, nothing more," Duncan said.

Razor leaned in a little closer, "What you don't seem to understand is it doesn't matter. I have you now, and I'm going to get to the truth of who you are and who you work for. If I have to rip it from you screaming at me, then so be it. This right here is happening, and you are powerless to stop it," he said.

Chapter 12

S anchez arrived at Remar IV, and her ship docked in a position outside the sensor range.

"So that's where he went," she said quietly.

"I am unable to scan the surface with any accuracy, Agent Sanchez, as we are beyond even my long-range sensors," the AI told her.

"I'm aware of that. I just wanted to take a look before we venture any further. Chances are Duncan was shot down as he approached, so I'm just being cautious, that's all," she said.

"Thank you for your consideration."

"It's not just for you. If I find Duncan down there, we're going to need a way off the planet. I can't go having you shot to pieces now, can I?" she clarified.

"Agent Sanchez, if I had feelings, I would be hurt by that comment."

"It's a good thing you don't have any then, isn't it?"

"What are your orders, Agent Sanchez?"

"Take us in but keep a stealth shield up. If they shot Duncan down, I'm not going to make the same mistake. Put us down close to where he landed," she said.

"Copy that, taking us in now," the AI replied.

Duncan braced himself for what was coming. All agents were trained in techniques to withstand torture, but they all also knew that no one could last forever under sustained pressure from a dedicated and talented torturer. These were a breed apart. To know how to reach a person's limits and then go beyond without shutting down that person so they got nothing out of him was a true skill. If they went too far, the victim would tell them anything just to stop the pain.

Knowing just how far to go to get the required results wasn't easy. He was about to learn just how good this Razor was.

"Now, we're going to start off with something basic just to get things moving. Let's start off with your name, shall we?" Razor said, coming to stand next to him once more.

"It's Michael Wiseman," Duncan said.

"Well done, that wasn't so hard now, was it?"

Duncan knew they could verify that by simply checking the ID implant in his forearm. It could be changed at any time to display whatever identity the agent needed. Duncan had had time before he was captured to activate the Michael Wiseman ID.

Razor ran a scanner over his forearm to read his chip to confirm his ID.

"Well done, you got one right," Razor said. He seemed to be enjoying himself far too much.

"Let's try something a bit harder. Who do you work for?"

"Universal Travel, I already told you that."

A sudden searing pain ran through his entire body. It caught him by surprise, so he had no chance to prepare for it.

It seemed to hit every part of his body at the same time, and there was nothing he could do about it. Seconds stretched into what felt like minutes of excruciating pain until, suddenly, it was gone. The relief was almost as overwhelming as the sudden pain had been, and it left Duncan breathing heavily until he regained his composure.

Razor was standing directly in front of him, watching Duncan closely like a predator eyeing its prey.

"What do you want from me?" Duncan shouted breathlessly, keeping to his cover identity. "I've told you the truth; what more can I do?"

"You can start by telling me the truth. You see, although your ID chip says you're Michael Wiseman, I already know that agents can have false IDs inserted into their chips. Now, are you going to tell me who you work for? Believe me, I have all day, and I'll keep asking until I get the truth," Razor said.

"You don't want the truth; you want an answer that fits your perception of who you think I am. I've already told you the truth," Duncan said. He was giving himself enough time to isolate the pain receptors in his brain. It was the only way he was going to survive the next few minutes.

"Well, that is partially true. You see, I already have an idea of who you work for, I just need you to confirm it on the record. So, let's continue, shall we?" Razor said and activated the chair again.

Duncan felt the full effect of the searing pain again coursing through his entire body, and he screamed louder this time. Sweat broke out across his forehead from the agony his body was straining to endure, and tears filled his tightly clamped-shut eyes.

Relief came after what seemed like hours, and he slumped in the chair, his head falling forward so his chin rested on his chest. His mind raced, trying to figure out what had just happened. He could control the pain receptors in his brain to nullify pain in extreme conditions which enabled him to fight through it. This time it hadn't worked. Without that control, he was at his torturer's mercy. That didn't worry him as much as the loss of control did. He prided himself on always having control over his body and his emotions. It was what set him apart from everyone else. It also isolated him to a great deal of what others had, but he was willing to accept that to be able to do his job.

Without that control, he was just like everyone else.

"Oh, I forgot to mention. While you were asleep, shall we say, you were injected with a drug that heightens your senses. It stimulates your nerve endings so that every sensation you feel is fully enhanced, almost visceral," Razor said with a cruel smile. He frowned and then said, "Forgive me, I forgot to ask a question first. Now, let's try that again. Who do you work for?"

"How many times do I have to tell you? I work for UniTrav. Contact them, they'll confirm it," Duncan pleaded, and this time he felt fear, real fear. There was no indication of when the pain would come. He hadn't seen his torturer activate any kind of switch or anything like that. It just hit him. Knowing that it could arrive at any second heightened the anticipation and fear.

"As many times as it takes for me to get to the truth. Trust me, you'll tell me what I need soon enough. When you've had enough of this, you'll tell me," Razor replied.

Duncan knew the truth in that. No one ever lasted forever under torture. Inevitably everyone reached their limits and gave up what they were trying to hide. Duncan had no idea what his limits were or how much he could endure because he'd always been able to mask pain and continue through it when others would have broken. Without that barrier, that control, he had no idea how soon he would break. He just knew that he would, and that scared him almost as much as the torture itself.

Chapter 13

Sanchez's ship landed near the crash site of Duncan's ship. On the way down, the AI had performed sensor sweeps of the compound, and she now knew how many people were inside and where exactly they were keeping Duncan.

"You cannot enter that camp on your own, Agent Sanchez. The odds of you getting Commander Pryde and escaping are fourteen thousand, six hundred and ninety-seven to one," the AI informed her.

"I agree; it doesn't sound good. I'm open to suggestions here. Come on, Ship, you're supposed to be the brainy one in this act. Give me some options," she replied.

"I have informed the government of this colony that there is a terrorist training base at this location and that they are planning a strike on this planet," the AI said.

"How does that help me get inside?" she asked.

"I will create a diversion on the opposite side of the compound, giving you the opportunity to enter from here. After you reach Commander Pryde, you will exit the same way. By this time, the tac team, which is being sent to hit this compound, should arrive. It will give you the extra cover under which you can safely exit the compound."

"I'm impressed. You did all that just now?" she asked.

"I ran through various simulations of strategies on our way here, and when I saw what you were planning, I initiated the scenario with the highest rate of success."

"What are my odds now? Wait, don't tell me. I'm not sure I want to know," she said, stopping herself short.

"The odds have greatly increased in your favour, Agent Sanchez," the AI said.

"What condition is Duncan in?" she asked. She knew his vitals were being monitored constantly both by her ship's AI and back at base by Goodchild.

"His heart rate is extremely high, as is his blood pressure. He is under extreme duress, it seems. What can cause such an effect, Agent Sanchez?"

"Torture, he's being tortured," she replied.

When the pain finished, Duncan almost passed out. He'd never felt pain like it before in his entire life.

He looked up at the calm face of his torturer, who seemed as relaxed as if this was just another day at the office.

"That was level two. Remember what I said about no one ever surviving past three? Well, you're almost there. If I were you, I would seriously start to reconsider what I was doing. Surely you can't be enjoying this, so why not tell me what I want to know? Do you honestly think your boss gives a fuck about you? The first rule an operative learns is that if you get captured, you will be disavowed. No one is coming to rescue you; they've probably issued your obit to the media already. You don't owe them a thing, so why not tell me what I want to know?" Razor said.

Duncan lifted his head off his chest, looked him in the eyes, and said, "You have the wrong guy. I work for UniTrav."

"Okay, last chance. Let's see how you like level three," Razor told him.

Duncan tried to resist, tried to brace himself, but it was useless. The pain hit his central nervous system like a freight train, lighting up every synapse in his brain. Every nerve ending lit up like a Christmas tree on December twenty-fifth.

A scream that was pure feral in nature was ripped from deep inside him as his entire body went rigid, every single muscle tightening to an impossible degree as he strained to contain it.

Willing it to end, hoping more like it, he tried to endure, not to give in. His life, his existence now, was nothing but pain.

He was still screaming when it suddenly ended, and his body relaxed once more, now completely drenched in sweat.

"Wow! That was intense," Razor said, laughing almost hysterically as he jumped from one foot to the other. He stopped and leaned down to look Duncan in the face, lifting his head up to see his eyes better.

"I think we've had enough for the day, don't you? I've had enough, anyway. We can continue where we left off tomorrow morning, bright and early. It'll give you some time to think things over and reconsider your situation," he said, then turned and headed for the opening.

"Take him back to his tent; keep a guard on him. He is to have nothing but bread and water until our next session tomorrow," he said to the man standing guard at the opening.

The restraints on his hands and feet were released, and he tried to stand. His legs were so weak he fell to the ground and lay there, unable to move. Two men grabbed an arm each and hoisted him up, then dragged him from the tent and across the compound to another, which they entered, and threw him onto a camp bed at the far end.

Through misty eyes, he watched them leave, laughing at his condition, and he thought he heard one say something about another one biting the dust.

When he was alone, he lay there, weakened and feeling defenceless, which filled him with shame. He was at his worst, almost at breaking point, which he knew was the intention of his torturer. He'd been left to think about what was coming tomorrow, and the expectation of more of the same as today would help to instil in him a feeling of absolute dread and terror.

It was working, too, as he felt tears running down his cheeks both from relief at the pain ceasing momentarily and from fear, for he knew it would return soon.

His loss of control had taken a toll greater than he could have imagined. Somehow, he had to find the strength within him to endure tomorrow, for one thing Razor had gotten right was that no one was coming to rescue him. He was alone, disavowed, so this was his fate. What bothered him was why.

Why had they gone to all this trouble to find him, lure him all the way out here to torture him? What did they hope to learn apart from who he worked for? Were they planning on hitting the Ministry? That made no sense at all because if they were planning something like that, they would already know who the target was. This was something else, and it smacked of revenge, but revenge for what? During his career, he had made some enemies, so which of them would be capable of mounting an operation of this magnitude?

He feared that even if he did learn the truth, he would be unable to act on it.

Fatigue took over, and he felt his eyes closing. He gave in and allowed darkness to engulf his aching body. In seconds, he entered the blessed sanctuary of sleep.

Chapter 14

S anchez waited in the dark where the ship had landed.

The sky had closed in on them as the sun dipped below the horizon. She was timing things so that they coordinated with the tac team arriving.

Her ship had left her to deliver the diversion on the other side of the compound, and again it was all timed for the maximum effect.

She had checked her sidearm several times as her anxiety made her a little jumpy. Any second now, and she was going to make her move.

An explosion at the far end of the compound lit up the sky with a fiery demonstration of power and chaos as lights suddenly went on around the camp. Figures streamed out of their tents, moving to the far end of the compound to see what caused the disturbance.

This was her signal to move in.

Duncan was jolted awake by the blast, and for a second, he was completely disoriented.

Looking around, he took in his surroundings, and then his memory of what had happened returned in all its painful glory.

Getting up from the camp bed proved difficult as he was still weak from his ordeal. He wasn't injured in any way, just very weak from the drugs they'd injected him with, plus the pain he endured, which would sap anyone's resistance.

Getting to his feet after falling over from the cot, he looked around to see what he could use as a weapon.

The tent was empty. He had to rely on his own ability. Creeping as quietly as he could to the entrance of his tent, he slowly pushed aside the tent flap to peer outside.

People running past his tent caught his attention, and something else. His guard had vacated his post, probably like the rest of the camp, and had gone to see what the commotion was.

Leaving the tent but keeping out of sight of the others, he made his way around the other side and set off in the opposite direction to which they were heading. If they were going one way, it made sense to make use of their confusion and go in the other direction.

That was as far as he got with planning his escape. He had no idea how he would get off the planet once he was clear of the compound or how to survive outside in the outback. All he knew was he would rather die out there than remain here and allow them to continue their torture of him.

His plan was working fine until one of the men caught sight of him and raised the alarm.

More of them turned to see what their comrade meant and saw him hobbling in the opposite direction. Three of them turned to intercept him and were on him in a flash. In his weakened state, he was no match for them, yet still, he struggled to free himself from their clutches.

He elbowed one in the face and stamped down hard on the calf of another, hoping to break the leg, but a blow to the back of his head dropped him to his knees.

Stars danced before his eyes, and he was on the verge of collapse when the two men at his sides suddenly fell to the ground leaving a mist of blood in the air. He turned his head to see the final one behind him being knocked over as a bullet hit him in the throat, sending blood spurting from his neck.

Duncan looked up, unsure of what exactly had just happened, when he saw Sanchez appear like an apparition in a dream.

"Are you real?" he asked, pushing her helping hand away, not sure if this was all part of some elaborate plan of his torturer to give him false hope before ripping it away from him to demoralise him even further.

"Yes, Duncan, it's me. I'm here to take you home," she said and grabbed him again to lift him off the ground.

"Home, yes," he stammered, "let's go home," he added.

More explosions ripped tents apart at the far end of the compound as grenades fell from beyond the perimeter. Gunfire followed, and they both saw bodies fall as they were hit.

"Come on, Duncan. Time for us to leave," Sanchez said.

The tac team had arrived.

Razor woke from a satisfying slumber at the first sound of the diversion. He quickly got dressed, pulling on his pants as he listened to the chaos outside.

Having no idea what was happening, his first thought was to investigate. As he exited his tent, he saw the men and women of the camp rushing toward where the explosion had occurred.

Grabbing an assault rifle from a rack outside another tent, he followed the crowd. He was halfway through the camp when he saw someone pointing in the opposite direction. He turned to see what had caught their attention and saw the man he knew as Michael Wiseman running away.

"Oh no, you don't," he said and turned to run after him. He slowed his pace when he saw three others capture him. He watched the spirited defence Wiseman put up, which was quickly quelled as he fell to a blow to the back of his head.

The two men flanking him were quickly dropped, followed by the third, and he saw who was the reason.

"Well, hello there. Who do we have here?" he said as he picked up his pace toward them.

More explosions behind him stopped him in his tracks as he saw a tac team advancing on the camp.

That made his mind up for him. He let Wiseman go as he now focussed his attention on his own escape.

There was a shuttle over to his right parked just outside the perimeter, along with other vehicles, an assortment of cars, ATVs, and more shuttles. Not waiting to see if the attack would be repelled or not, he was going to get out before his boss found out Wiseman had escaped before giving them anything. That was a conversation for another day and when he was a very long way away.

Chapter 15

Sanchez helped Duncan out of the compound and led him to where her ship was waiting. Once she had him through the hatch, she ordered her AI to take off.

Duncan was in a sorry state. There were no visible signs of trauma, but it was clear he had been put through a wringer. She was sad to see him looking so despondent and afraid. He kept jumping at every noise and was constantly looking around, staring into the corners at things only his tortured mind could see.

Laying him down on a bunk behind the command chair, she said, "Try and get some rest. We'll be home soon."

She felt a wave of extreme sadness wash over her as she saw him curl up into a foetal position.

"Ship, get us out of here and back to Terra II. Duncan needs help right now," she said sternly.

"Copy that, Agent Sanchez, making the jump now," replied the AI, and she felt the familiar surge as the engines powered them through the hyperspace window.

Razor had exited the planet in the shuttle and saw another ship enter a hyperspace window and then vanish.

There was no doubt in his mind that Pryde was on board that ship, but seeing as how they had shot down his own ship, which had the tracker on it, they were left with no way to track him now.

He had only one thing in his favour. He had a name, which probably wasn't his real name, but he also had a place of employment. It was somewhere to start, at least. Maybe he could learn who he really was from their records.

He set course for Terra II and made the jump to hyperspace.

MI7 HQ, Terra II

Sanchez deposited Duncan at a secret medical facility called Section Two and was on the way to see C when she was intercepted by Goodchild.

"Good work bringing Duncan back," she said, stopping her from going any further.

"Shouldn't I report this to C?" Sanchez asked.

"No, this is strictly off the books. He is keeping the review board occupied while Duncan handles the investigation."

"Plausible deniability?" Sanchez asked.

"Exactly," Goodchild replied. "How is he?" she asked, changing the subject.

"Doc says he'll make a full recovery, but he needs complete rest. His body will heal pretty fast, but he's concerned about the emotional trauma he went through during the torture session."

"I can't imagine what he went through, but he must have gone through hell," Goodchild commented.

"We'll just have to give him time to recover," Sanchez said. "What do you want me to do in the meantime?"

"Stand ready. I'm looking into who captured him and why. As soon as I have something for you, I'll be in touch."

"Okay, I'll stay with Duncan to keep an eye on him," Sanchez said, then left, heading back to Section Two.

Razor put down at a spaceport in the centre of New London. He didn't want to attract too much attention. He found a hotel that was out of the way and booked a room for the time being until he knew what he was going to do next.

He accessed an encrypted comm channel and made the dreaded call.

"Why are you on Terra II?" the voice asked before he even had time to speak. It scared him more than he liked to admit, the fact they knew exactly where he was.

"I have an update for you," he said, a little rattled by the knowledge they could be watching.

"If you are going to say anything other than you have completed your mission, you know the consequences," the voice pointed out.

Razor took a calming breath and said, "He was rescued by a military tac team before he broke."

"I see, so you didn't get anything useful on record."

"No, he got away before I could get anything concrete," he replied a little tentatively.

"Okay, we'll take care of him later. I'm giving you a chance to redeem yourself. Report to Haltor tomorrow. All the details will be sent to your PIN," the voice said and closed the call.

He had a moment's grace then until he was on the move again tomorrow, so he chose to spend it wisely.

Chapter 16

Haltor

The destruction of the base that nestled in the shadow of the cliff had been part of a plan but necessary, and the work being done there had been salvaged.

Knowing that the attack was coming had given them time to move all the sensitive material being produced there to another location on the other side of the planet. The work continued after the brief interruption and was the most ambitious project to date.

The new site was on an island off the east coast of the largest landmass on the planet. It was owned by a secretive billionaire who was rumoured to be associated with several criminal organisations, but nothing was ever proved. Money has a way of hiding facts and obliterating accountability.

Razor had received orders to report there and leave the agent to others. He was to take part in the new program, which he knew nothing of. Knowing better than to question, he took his ship and headed to his new location.

As he approached the island, he could see several small buildings that resembled dwellings and a couple of larger ones that could be offices. There was a massive pool near the main palatial residence, large enough to host swimming galas.

It was obvious whoever this guy was, he wasn't even attempting to hide his wealth. He might as well hold up a sign that read, 'Here lives the wealthiest man on this planet.'

He landed his ship on the pad designated for him and walked toward the main residence, where he was greeted by three men. They were his welcoming committee.

"Welcome to Lassiter Island," the man in front said, the other two flanking him and watching his every move like hungry guard dogs. "If you'd like to follow me, I'll take you to the main house where Mister Lassiter is expecting you," he said, ushering Razor in front of him.

The main house was built in the Georgian style and was four floors high with a large double-fronted entrance that stood over two metres high.

Three stone steps led up to the front door. Guards armed with assault rifles stood on either side of the doors. As they approached, they moved apart to allow them entry.

"Mister Lassiter is in the lounge. Go ahead, he's expecting you," his guide said, then stepped aside.

Razor walked into the lounge, rich stained wooden floors stretched before him, and luxurious white leather furniture was placed decoratively to enhance the image of comfort. Paintings adorned the walls, and a white marble fireplace was to his right, where a tall man stood leaning nonchalantly with his elbow on the mantle.

"You must be Razor," he said. "Intriguing name. Do you know why you are here?"

"I go where I'm told," he replied.

"Let me fill you in a little then. The group I work for, the same as you, is developing a weapon here. Something we intend on selling to the highest bidder. First, though, we have to demonstrate it. You are here to lead the operation for that demonstration."

"What is this weapon?" Razor asked. He figured if he was to deliver it to a target, he best know what it did and what risks he would be facing doing so.

"Have you ever heard of a bioweapon called Omega Five?" Lassiter asked.

Razor nodded as his face froze. He knew it by reputation and also that there had been a breach at a facility that was still manufacturing it against strict orders from the Coalition that all samples be destroyed.

"Good, well, we are producing some here, but we are simply making the base virus. What we manufacture here is capable of destroying all life on a planet, stripping it bare so that it can be seeded with whatever life forms the customer deems fit."

Razor was horrified at the implications of this. They were making something that could completely wipe out all life on a planet. The enormity of that was astronomical.

"Can you see the potential in this? No more terraforming. You simply pick a planet, use this, and then seed it with whatever life you want. Then you have a ready-made home for billions of people."

"What about the other side of the coin?" Razor asked.

"That's where you come in. I want you to deliver a batch of this to a location you'll be told later and then come back here. It's as simple as that," Lassiter told him, all his previous excitement gone as it was time to get down to business.

"I take it you've picked a target that is already inhabited for your demonstration?" Razor said, stating the obvious.

Lassiter looked at him, shrugged, then said, "How else would we demonstrate its potential? Don't worry; we've minimised the fallout. There should be no more than a few million casualties."

"A few million?" Razor asked, keeping his voice under control.

"Yes, it's a difficult balance. If you keep the numbers too low, they can chalk it off to a natural disaster or some other phenomenon. If you hit the really high numbers, they call you a mass murderer. But, if you hit that sweet spot, they take notice just enough to know you're serious, and they can't put any kind of spin on it on the news channels. I think we have the perfect spot for our demonstration."

Razor nodded, not sure what to say. He had to go along with this. The consequences of refusing meant he would be on the run for the rest of his extremely short life. He had no morals about killing. He'd done it often enough. Most of his kills were either under contract or combat conditions. He had always tried to keep collateral damage to a minimum. Killing someone who knew what the risks were was acceptable, but killing innocent bystanders had always left a bitter taste in his mouth.

Who were these people who could erase so many lives with the ease of deleting numbers on a data file? What's more, how did he ever get mixed up with them?

"You look slightly perplexed. Is there something wrong?" Lassiter asked, picking up on him feeling uncomfortable.

Steeling himself, he said, "No, sir. I'm fine."

"Good, then we have the sample all ready for you, so you can leave right away. All the details of the target have been transferred to your ship's AI, and the sample is already on board. We have inserted it into a missile which you fire into the atmosphere as soon as you're in orbit. As soon as that is done, return here. We will have more work for you," Lassiter explained.

"Copy that," he replied. They were giving him no time to think about this, which was probably for the best. With a nod, he left the lounge and was escorted back to his ship.

Chapter 17

Rideleus III

The hyperspace window opened, and Razor's ship passed through back into normal space.

He was in the Rideleus star system, and his target was the third planet. As he approached, he was struck with the familiarity to that of his home world, Cerean. Clear blue oceans covered over half the planet, with landmasses that were home to exciting cities and lush greenery—and he was here to destroy it all.

As he entered orbit, the Flight Control Centre wanted to know his registration and reason for visiting Rideleus III, to which he stalled by giving them a false vehicle ID. It would only take them a few seconds to verify he was lying to them, so he had to act fast.

He fired the missile manually, aiming to place it in the atmosphere. As soon as the missile was away, he ordered the ship to open another hyperspace window and travelled through it.

He decided against running sensors on the planet or connecting to their data banks as he thought knowing how many lives he'd just taken would compromise his ability to perform his job. Now he was glad to be away from there and heading back to where he came from. The cloud was self-replicating so that it would spread much faster and survive the blast of the explosion.

The effects would start to be felt quite quickly, but the full effects would take a little longer.

Coalition Council HQ, Terra II

A meeting had been called for the defence council the moment the incident on Rideleus III was reported.

The effects of the virus had begun as early as a few hours after the ship had fired the missile into the atmosphere. People started to feel ill, and then the deaths began, followed by the destruction of wildlife and, finally, plant life. Pretty soon, it was obvious the entire planet was affected, and there was nothing to stop it from being totally wiped out of life, all life.

President Parris took control of the meeting the moment he sat down.

"What intel do we have on this incident?" he asked, getting right to the point.

"We tasked a ship to fly past and gather scans from the surface, sir. It appears that everyone is dead, sir," replied an aide.

This sent a cold shiver around the room as they all took in the enormity of those words.

"How many were on that planet?" Parris asked.

"At the last census, sir, it was twenty-three million, eight hundred and forty-seven thousand, nine hundred and thirty-eight, sir," the aide said slowly,

Parris had his head lowered as he listened, his eyes closed. A single tear ran down from his left eye as grief for those lost souls hit him. Wiping that tear away, he looked up and took a deep breath.

"Do we know what can cause such an event? Was it natural, or did someone cause this to happen?" he asked.

"We have no way of knowing yet, sir," the aide replied.

"Why not?" Parris shouted, "Get someone out there, and get me some answers," he added.

He looked around the table and slapped his hand down, halting any other conversations.

"Why is Director Chambers not present?" he asked.

Secretary for Defence, James Marshall, said, "His department is under investigation for the incident on Haltor. I didn't think it appropriate that he attend this meeting, sir."

"Really, and who gave you the authority to make decisions like that, James, because I certainly didn't? This witch hunt you have going on against him and his department has to stop. They are a vital component of our intelligence network, and to sideline them like that compromises every effort we make going forward. You have allowed your loyalty to the CIA to influence your decision-making process, and if you insist on continuing like this, I'll have no recourse but to replace you and your entire staff. Is that clear?" Parris said, angrier than anyone had ever seen him.

Marshall looked at all the other faces around the table as his cheeks reddened from the rebuke. All eyes were firmly on him as they waited to see what he was going to do. Not one single person averted their eyes, which sent a clear message to him that they all knew what his agenda was, and they disapproved of it.

"Perfectly clear, Mister President. I'll have my staff notified this instant that their investigation has been terminated," he said.

"You do that. In the meantime, I want a starship sent there to get some answers. Send a team to the surface to see if it was a natural event or if something else was in play. You will need medical experts and whoever else needs to be there to find out what the hell happened. I doubt very much this was a naturally occurring event, but if it was, we need to know for future knowledge. If this was caused by something else, we need to know what it was, who did it, and why," Parris said. After a moment's pause, he asked, "Is there anything else, anything that I missed?"

When all he got back were blank stares, he said, "Right, meeting adjourned. Let's get to work, people. I want to be kept informed every step of the way."

He watched everyone leave, especially Marshall, who caught his eye with a glance of hatred that was poorly disguised. That reminded him to call Chambers to see if he knew anything and to inform him about the investigation being called off.

SecOps HQ

"Mister President, what do I owe the honour of this call?" C said.

"What do you know of the incident on Rideleus III?" he asked.

"I've been a little busy dealing with the investigation into my organisation, sir."

"You can ignore that now; I've dealt with it. I ordered Marshall to call it off. I need you to look into the incident I just mentioned. It is strange, and I need your input into what it might be. I'll send all the data we have gathered up to this point to you. When you've looked it through, let me know your thoughts. This could be big, and I have a bad feeling it could get worse."

"I'll get right on it, Mister President," C said, then signed off.

He felt relieved that the witch hunt had been called off, but he knew it was too early to relax fully. He had a feeling that Marshall wasn't finished with him just yet, or rather Solvig wasn't, or better yet, whoever Solvig worked for. He was certain there was a puppet master at play here; so far, all he'd seen were the puppets, but who was pulling the strings, he wondered.

That would have to wait for now. He had more urgent matters to attend to as he opened the data file Parris had sent him. He just hoped Duncan was fit enough to return to work. He had a feeling he was going to need him on this one.

Solvig excused himself from Marshall, saying he had things to attend to. Once he was clear, he accessed an encrypted comm channel and called an associate.

"I need you to do something for me. There has been a glitch in our plans, so I need you to eliminate a certain problem for us," he said cryptically.

"Give me the location and name of the target, and I'll get right on it," the voice on the other end said.

Solvig did as requested and closed the call. A smile crossed his face. The President may have stalled their plan to tie up the Ministry and put a target on their agent's back, but there were more ways to skin a cat.

Sometimes the most direct route was the simplest and most efficient.

Chapter 18

New London, Secret Med Facility

Duncan was getting restless in Section Two as he relaxed as part of his recuperation.

It had been three days since his arrival back on Terra II. Although MI7 was still not acknowledging his recent activities, and he remained on the inactive roster, C did everything he could behind the scenes to ensure he received the best medical treatment.

He was already recuperating from his ordeal; the wounds had been treated and were healing quickly due to the enhanced recovery processes used, but he still suffered mental anguish from being tortured.

His room was comfortable, with space enough to relax when he wasn't lying in bed. Monitors attached to the bio-bed kept his vital signs under surveillance around the clock.

He had begun to exercise to regain his mobility and strength. It was going to be an uphill struggle, but it wasn't the first time he'd been injured on the job. It was the first time he'd been tortured, though.

Being in control of his emotions, an ability he had been born with and perfected throughout his life, helped him recover faster from mental trauma than normal people. He could partition off feelings so they didn't impact his ability to make decisions. This time, however, he had to concentrate harder than ever before to compartmentalise those memories, those feelings of terror, of vulnerability. He even began to wonder if all this was worth it.

Several times he'd put his life on the line, been almost killed, and for what? To protect people who have never even heard of him, who were absolutely and completely unaware of what he'd done for them. Why should he continue to sacrifice everything he had to protect those who wouldn't even give him the time of day? Didn't he deserve a life of his own?

Since working with the Ministry, he had forsaken all friendships. The thought of family, a wife, and children was for others and not people like him. Yet more and more, he was beginning to wonder why not for him.

He was at a crossroads. Of that, he was painfully aware—whether to continue down this path he'd begun so many years ago or to step off and take another path. One where he put his own needs before all the millions of lives in the galaxy who seem to rely on him so much without even knowing who he was. He was beginning to actually look at a life beyond the Ministry, and he realised he didn't know what he'd do if he ever did take that step off the road.

This day was like all the others. He was woken by one of the nurses to start his physio before the doctors checked his progress. He was a high-value patient and was treated as such and kept incommunicado, his true identity a secret.

The Med Lab was on the banks of the river, and an alarm sounded as three attack boats approached.

Duncan was being checked out by the doctor when the alarm reverberated around the facility.

"What's that?" he asked when he heard it. The terrified expression on the doctor's face provided all the answers he needed.

Quickly, Duncan reached for his clothes in the wardrobe. He dressed in a hurry and shrugged into his holster. He checked his SAP10 for a full load, then replaced it in the holster.

"Doc, if you have any security staff, I would suggest you get them ready and armed. We're about to have some company," Duncan said, then rushed out of his room. He felt the rush of adrenaline flood his system, which he controlled, so it helped him fuel his actions rather than paralyse them with fear.

He had no proof the boats were there for him, but he had a good idea. After recent events, he was taking no chances about it and was getting ready to greet them, just in case.

The three boats sped toward the river bank, led by Mikal LaRoche in the first boat. He was a merc, as were all the others in the boats.

Dressed all in black combat gear and armed with ARX assault rifles, along with an assortment of other weapons, they headed for the facility.

Leaving the boats on the bank, they rushed toward the walls of the facility. Explosive charges were placed and then detonated, taking out a portion of the wall large enough for them to get through.

Security staff rushed to the scene of the intrusion and were met by overwhelming force. Bullets from the intruder's weapons shredded the bodies of the defending forces, dropping them in moments. Their path clear, the intruders entered.

LaRoche said, "Find him and kill him."

Duncan heard the gunfire and knew they had breached the facility. They were coming for him, and he had to be ready.

Who they were was still a mystery, but he was determined to find answers to his questions.

First, he had to survive the next few minutes, though.

He had to find somewhere that he could gather intel on his attackers to form a plan of attack.

He was on the third floor, and the breach had occurred on the ground level, so he had time to move. He was out of his room and running toward the elevator. He saw the lights go on as it was called.

He had hoped to get in before they called it. If he had planned this, he would have sent a team up in the elevator whilst the rest went up the stairs. That way, he would have every point of egress covered.

Seeing the elevator call button light up meant they had thought of the same thing.

He opened the door next to the elevator and took to the stairs, running up them, hoping to put some distance between them before the inevitable encounter.

As he powered up the stairs, he felt the strain of his recent injuries. He was feeling better but was still not one hundred percent. One flight up, and he was breathing harder than he should.

A door slammed up above him, followed by footsteps coming down. Looking up through the middle gap by the handrail, he saw several armed figures working their way down the stairs.

They must have landed on the roof to form a pincer movement and capture him between the two parts.

This made his task that much harder. On the landing, he opened the door and rushed through. He would have to find another way to get past them.

Chapter 19

The floor Duncan entered was another research level. Tables festooned with equipment and phials of various liquids that could be anything were seen through doors to rooms as he passed them by.

As soon as the shooting had started, the alarm had resounded throughout the entire hospital. All the personnel had fled for the exits to escape whatever the threat was.

Emergency exit doors had been left open, as everyone had escaped as fast as they could. Chairs had been tipped over, and tools and equipment discarded while still in use in some cases. The other patients who needed help were transported via gurneys or chairs to the exits, where they, too, were taken to safety.

He ran through the first corridor, passing several rooms, looking for a way out. As he reached an exit in the last room at the far end of the corridor, he looked back and saw figures enter the same floor.

Bullets came screaming at him, smashing through the glass walls of the room and splintering the door frame as he ducked through. Debris from the impacts were sent flying into the air, missing Duncan by a hair's breadth.

The door he'd gone through led to a fire escape ladder that was affixed to the wall. He glanced down through the metal ladder just in time to see an armed soldier aim his ARX up at him.

"Oh shit!" he shouted as he jumped back inside. Bullets followed him, tearing up the floor and ricocheting off the fire escape.

Out of the frying pan into the fire.

He now had to face those coming at him on this floor. He rolled onto his knees after diving back into the room and fired a few rounds into the group approaching him. He saw a mist of blood appear as one of his rounds plucked at an arm, spinning one soldier around.

As the others looked for cover in other glass-walled rooms, he did the same and dived behind a desk.

How could he get past these guys, he wondered as bullets peppered the desk he hunkered down behind? All he had was his SAP10, no grenades, no other means of defending himself, and cover that would soon disappear.

Getting his emotions under control, he dampened down his feelings to perform more efficiently. Having no fear meant he could do things that normal people would baulk at the mere thought of. He could take chances a rational person would think long and hard before committing to. He would do it without a second's hesitation, which was what he did next.

Standing up, he started to walk toward the entrance. Glimpsing a gunman peering around a desk he was using as cover, Duncan shot him through the eye. Blood jetted out the back of his head in a red gory stream, painting the floor behind him before he fell backwards.

Another soldier appeared and received the same treatment. He shot everyone who was brave enough to take a look as he walked purposefully toward the door to this floor.

Three of them gathered together near the door, rose up, and fired at him in a panic-fueled cacophony of gunfire. Bullets filled the air as they sprayed shells indiscriminately at him, hoping upon hope that at least one would stop this maniac.

Duncan just carried on walking, focussed entirely on his destination and the obstacles presenting themselves before him. His aim was perfect as there was no doubt, no fear, to cloud his judgment, so when he fired, he hit the target.

One shot took out the forehead of the nearest soldier to the aisle, sending him dropping back into his comrades. They collided, which sent their next bullets flying into the ceiling. Pieces of ceiling tiles rained down as each bullet smashed through it. Dust and pieces of debris showered the soldiers still standing before Duncan terminated them with a bullet each to their heads.

Duncan relieved the soldiers of ammunition and an ARX, giving him an increased chance of survival.

Leaving this floor, Duncan returned to the stairs and decided to go back down rather than escape through the roof. He needed to find out who these soldiers were and who sent them. If, in doing so, he was able to save the lives of the people who worked in this facility, it was all the more reason to do it.

He didn't have to go far to encounter the rest of the invading force.

La Roche heard the gunfire coming from the floor above as he entered the stairwell.

They had either found him or were clearing that floor to get to him. Either way, he didn't care much as long as it led to their target.

Rushing up the stone stairs, he followed his men, leading from the back. No point in putting his own life in danger when he had others whom he could put in front, especially in this stairwell where they could only travel at most two abreast.

He was behind three rows of two when a figure appeared in the doorway and opened fire with an ARX, cutting down the first two in seconds.

"Fall back," he shouted in earnest. The last thing he needed was to get killed on this mission.

The next two men fell before the onslaught before the rest had time to back down the stairs, and he began to panic. He fought through his own men to get to safety as more of them fell under the shooter's onslaught.

Some of them held their water and returned fire. Bullets struck the wall and door frame, sending debris and wood chips flying into the air, forcing the shooter back inside for a second. This gave them a chance to regroup and get back down to safety.

"Motherfucker!" La Roche shouted from the relative safety of the ground floor. "Find another way up to that floor and try to box the bastard in. We'll get him in a crossfire and finish this," he said. Half of whoever remained of his team left to find the alternative route to the upper floor as commanded.

This was turning out to be a lot harder than he had been led to believe. One man, indeed. Who the fuck was this guy?

Chapter 20

Sanchez had left Section Two to take a break. She'd spent almost all her time staying with Duncan to ensure he didn't do anything rash and stuck to his recovery regimen.

She was just returning when she saw the boats approaching from the water and a chopper landing on the roof of the facility.

"Oh, this can't be good," she said as she ran as fast as she could toward the facility.

As she neared the ground floor entrance, she drew her SAP10 and jacked the slide to inject a round into the breach. Through the glass-fronted window, she saw a group of armed men. There was blood smeared on the windows from the dead bodies littering the floor. She knew what they were there for, and it was nothing good.

They were after Duncan, that much was for sure. How they found him would be a question to be asked later. At the moment, her priority had to be keeping him safe. Running up to the entrance, she fired through the glass, dropping two of the men standing there, their focus on the stairwell. That soon changed when two of their numbers dropped from gunshots.

Caught off guard, they turned around to face this new threat, bringing up their ARX rifles to fire.

Sanchez dropped another one of them before she had to divert her run at them.

Bullets shattered more glass as they returned fire. Sanchez dove into a tuck and rolled to the side, coming up on one knee to fire again.

Her first shot struck one of the soldiers in the neck, severing his carotid. His eyes went wide in shock as he clamped a hand over the wound. Blood seeped through his fingers as he dropped his ARX to concentrate on trying to save his life.

La Roche saw his men go down from this new assault and turned his attention to it.

At that moment, Duncan saw his chance to act. Rushing down the stairs, he reached the landing as the soldiers were caught, not knowing which way to turn first.

He shot the first two men he saw, dropping them with head shots. This caused panic in the rest, as they knew they were now caught in a deadly crossfire, the very same thing they had hoped to catch him in.

Outside, Sanchez continued firing, using the moment's confusion to drop two more.

There was now complete panic inside as the soldiers were being hit from both sides with seeming no cover in sight.

La Roche saw this and knew this mission was over. They had failed, and the only thing to do now was escape to live and fight another day, a creed he lived by. Pulling two grenades from his belt, he primed them and tossed one toward the stairwell and the other through the shattered glass front of the building, then dashed for the exit at the side.

Sanchez saw the explosive come hurtling toward her through the shattered windows. Getting to her feet, she ran away as fast as she could.

The grenade hit the ground and bounced several times before detonating.

The explosion hit her hard in the back, lifting her off her feet and tossing her several feet across the ground. Landing hard, she rolled a few times before stopping, as breathless as she was stunned.

Pain coursed through her body, the effects of the blast. She saw stars dancing before her eyes as she tried to get up. Her head felt like an entire band of miners were trying to hammer their way out of her skull, and she fell back, her head spinning.

Blood seeped from a cut on her head, down her forehead, and into her eyes, forcing her to close them. The dizziness took away what was left of her senses, and she passed out.

Duncan saw the grenade tossed his way. There was no way for him to evade it.

While it was still in mid-air, he swotted it away back into the entrance area. The blast took out the rest of the windows, sending shards of glass across the ground outside just after the other detonation.

Duncan pressed his back against the wall inside the stairwell to shield himself from the blast.

Whoever was left standing on the other side of the door was caught in the blast and torn apart. Blood and body parts were sent across the area, painting it all in blood.

When the blast had dissipated, Duncan peered around the door jamb to see the carnage, and he saw it dispassionately. They had brought violence to this medical facility; they had killed innocent people, so he felt no guilt for having caused their deaths.

Looking around, he couldn't see the man in charge. He'd only seen him briefly, yet he'd recognised him immediately—using his own men as cover, leading from the back—the worst kind of leader. A quick scan of the bodies told him he wasn't there, which could only mean he'd escaped. Typical reaction for one of his kind, putting his life above others.

There must be a side exit that he'd used to escape, probably after he'd tossed the grenades.

He dashed for the exit in pursuit; he wasn't going to allow him to escape. There were too many questions he needed answers to, and he was the only lead he had.

Chapter 21

Leaving the facility, Duncan looked to see which way his target had gone. Seeing him fleeing toward where the boats were moored, he took off after him. He had to sprint as fast as he could to close the gap between them. There was at least a few hundred yards gap, and he could see him almost at the mooring post where the small boats had been left.

La Roche was signalling for the three people left to guard the boats to all get into one and prepare to shove off. In an act of desperation, Duncan fired his ARX on the run, spraying bullets at the fleeing figure. His aim was off, and the bullets shredded the nearest boat's gunwales instead of the fleeing figure. It got everyone's attention, though, and the men on the boats returned fire.

He continued running and firing as his target reached one of the boats. The rest of the men had congregated on this one boat, and as soon as he leaped over the side into it, they cast off. The high-power engine sent a spume of spray over the dock as it sped away.

Not giving up, Duncan ran and leaped over the side of one of the other two boats and started the engine. In less than a minute, he was giving chase down the river, which led to the open sea a few miles away.

He pushed the engine to the max, opening up all the throttles to get as much speed out of it as he possibly could. The people on that boat were the only lead to who was behind this heinous attack. He had to catch them; he had no choice. Failure was simply not an option.

"Who is that guy?" one of the men on the boat asked as they looked at the chasing boat behind them.

"That's the guy we were supposed to off," La Roche said through gritted teeth.

"Plan not going so well then," the guy sneered. The sarcasm was not lost on La Roche. He just didn't know how he'd explain this failure to his boss. Maybe he wouldn't have to.

"Shoot that bastard," he said, and two of the others went to the aft of the boat to lean on the side as they targeted the boat behind them with their ARXs.

Bullets traced a path through the water to Duncan's boat, but he wasn't there. Turning the wheel hard to port, he evaded the gunfire. Still, a few stray shells caught the rear panel of his boat as he turned away.

Resting his own ARX on the side of the pilot house, Duncan steered the boat with one hand as he fired the rifle with the other.

His salvo raked the aft section of the boat, rising up from the waterline to just over the edge, where it struck one of the gunmen in the face, destroying it in a gory splash of red.

The man screamed as the bullets hit his face, pulverising it before his body dropped back inside the boat.

He closed the gap between the two boats a little more.

The remaining soldier on the aft of the boat fired back at him. Bullets struck the back of the boat, chipping away at his meagre cover.

Duncan had one grenade remaining, so he primed it and tossed it unerringly into the back of the boat in front.

Panic widened the eyes of the men standing there as they realised their fate. The remaining soldier dived overboard on the port side, and the driver was about to do the same when La Roche grabbed him and pulled him in front of him as a human shield.

The grenade detonated, destroying the rear section of the boat in a fireball that sprayed burning shrapnel and parts of the vessel high into the air before coming to a sizzling rest in the water. Within seconds, the boat began to sink beneath the surface.

La Roche pushed the battered dead body of the driver off him and looked back into the cold hard stare of Duncan's eyes. When he saw he had no choice but to abandon the boat, he leaped over the side into the water and began to swim for it.

"Really, you're going to try and outswim a speed boat?" Duncan said as he pushed the throttles forward, giving the engine a push. He was soon alongside the swimming merc, keeping pace.

"Do you need a lift?" he asked.

Stopping swimming to tread water, La Roche reached up a hand for him to pull him out of the water.

Duncan grabbed his hand and immediately felt the other man plant his feet against the side of the boat and heave back, hoping to drag him into the water with him.

Jamming his right foot against the rail, he leaned back, preventing the move, and brought his SAP10 up to aim it at his face.

"Shall we try that again, or should I shoot you now?" he said.

"Get fucked!" La Roche spat the words at him defiantly.

"Suit yourself," Duncan said and smashed the butt of his SAP10 into the face of the man in the water. The blow stunned him long enough for him to grab a hold of his suit and drag him aboard. He turned him face down and snapped a pair of cuffs on his wrists.

"Maybe now we might get somewhere," he said as he turned the boat back to shore.

Chapter 22

SecOps HQ

"So that's one of them?" C observed as they looked at La Roche through the one-way glass of the interview room.

"That's him, sir," Duncan replied.

"Let's go in and see what we can see."

The interview room was just a bare room with a desk and chairs arranged around it. La Roche was on one side, and C and Duncan went to sit on the opposite side.

"Who sent you to try and kill this man here?" C asked, indicating Duncan at his side.

"I'll have my one call now, please. I know my rights," La Roche replied, leaning back in the chair and folding his arms across his chest.

"You think you have rights? Where do you think you are? This isn't a police station or any form of local authority base.

You're being held here under Section Eighty of the Prevention of Terrorism Act; I can keep you here as long as I want. You have no rights under this act, which means no one knows where you are, and I can do whatever I need to find out what I need from you," C said just as confidently.

This had the effect C wanted. The man sitting across from him visibly shrank as the reality of his predicament dawned on him.

Steeling himself, La Roche sat up straight before saying, "You've got nothing on me, and I can't tell you what you want to know because I don't know anything," he said.

"If you don't want us to probe your mind, then tell us everything you do know," C said.

La Roche swallowed hard, then said, "I don't know what you want me to say. I was given the hit over a call. The voice was altered, so I couldn't even tell you if the caller was a man or woman."

"Was this the first time you received such a call?" C probed.

"No, I've worked for this person several times."

"What kind of work? Is it always wet work, or do they employ you for other tasks?"

"No, it's always wet work."

"I want a list of jobs you completed for this person, including names of targets, times, and locations."

Shaking his head, La Roche said, "I can't do that."

"Why?"

"You have no idea who this is, nor do I, but I'll tell you one thing. They have a reach that extends everywhere. How else would we know your boy here was the target? If this is a secret agency of some kind, how did they know where he'd be and enough about him to know he was a threat to them? Think about that for a second. If they have that kind of reach, that kind of power, then they can reach me in here or wherever you decide to put me. They know who you are. They know everything about you."

Duncan and his boss exchanged glances. C looked back at La Roche and then said, "Thanks, that'll be all for now. You've been a great help. I'll be sure to put that into my report."

"Wait, what? You have to report this?" La Roche said, his face scrunching in confusion.

"Of course I do. You know how command structure works. Everyone has a boss, and we all report up the chain of command to our individual bosses. Don't you worry, though. I'll make sure they know what a help you've been in this. Someone will be along shortly to escort you to a safe place," C said as he got to his feet.

"I'm a fucking dead man. You killed me. I'm a dead man," La Roche kept saying, looking around the room like a caged animal.

Leaning on the tabletop and looking him straight in the eye, C said, "Then give me something I can work with, and I'll keep you safe."

"You think you can go after these people? Are you mad? You're insane if you think that. They hold all the cards. They are the ones with the power, not you. You just think you hold it, but it's an illusion. It's what they allow you to think, nothing more."

"Give me something I can use against them to bring them down. It's the only way you'll truly be safe."

When C saw the man falter, caught between his loyalty through fear for his employer and fear of a penal colony for life, he pushed further. "What choice do you have? If your claim that they'll get to you is correct, then your only chance here is to give me what I want or simply wait to be killed. It's entirely up to you," he said, giving him no choice at all, really.

Duncan was at the door, ready to leave as C backed away from the table in preparation for joining him when La Roche said, "Okay, what do you need?"

"A full list of times, dates, and locations of targets. Maybe from that, we can learn who benefitted from your actions, and we can then find who is behind all of this," C replied.

La Roche nodded in defeat.

"Add it to your PIN, and it'll be collected before you leave," C said, then the two of them left the room.

As Duncan closed the door behind them, he said, "You're pretty good at that, sir."

"Why do you sound so impressed?" C asked.

"I sometimes forget you were once a handler for the Ministry before taking over the reins of power, sir."

"Yes, many of my tasks back then were interrogation. You see, I know how to read people. Well, most people, that is. You, my boy, are still a mystery to me, a puzzle, but a puzzle I will solve one day. I'm sure of that."

"I have no idea what you mean, sir. I'm just doing my job," Duncan replied.

"Yes, well, before we do anything else, I want the doc to have a final look at you before signing you fit for duty. Just a formality, I'm sure, but better to be safe than sorry."

"Copy that, sir. I'll report to him directly," Duncan replied and left his boss to return to his office alone.

Chapter 23

Duncan entered the Med Lab and saw Sanchez sitting on a bio bed in one of the rooms.

"Come to visit me?" she asked, her eyes brightening at seeing him enter.

After the return to HQ, Duncan had relaxed his control over his emotions, allowing them to filter through to almost normal levels again. He smiled when he saw her sitting up, actually pleased to see she was alright.

"In a way, yes. I was here for a quick check-up so the doc could sign me off and back on the active roster list. How're you feeling? Any after-effects?" he replied.

"Just a few extra bruises, nothing major. Doc says I'm shaken up a bit, but I should be okay to return to duty," she said, stepping down from the bio bed to come over to him.

"How're you? Are you getting back to normal, whatever that is for you?" she asked.

"I feel fine, better than I should, I suppose. It helps to have control over my emotions like I do. I can dampen down any trauma that arises over the incident."

"Incident. Duncan, you were tortured, and if you keep hiding your feelings over it, you'll cause more problems later. You have to face it and deal with it so you can heal properly. If you don't, there'll come a time when you're in the field, and you won't be able to control it, and worst-case scenario, people could die, including you. For God's sake Duncan, deal with this before it's too late."

He saw the concern in her eyes. It was real. She felt for him, so why didn't he feel the same way about himself or her? Why was he so ignorant of people's feelings toward him? Did he care, or was he immune? Had he kept his feelings shut off for so long that he was now incapable of feeling anything?

A slight nod was the only acknowledgement he could give that he'd even heard what she'd said to him before he moved away silently in search of the doctor.

"Wait up, I'll come with you," she said, following him.

"You don't need to. I won't be long," he replied over his shoulder without looking at her. "I'll catch you later," he said, striding off to find the doctor. He didn't want to have to deal with that at the moment. He had to try and focus on the job at hand. Sanchez had been a distraction since the very first moment of their working together, and she continued to be even now. He must do his best to separate that from his mind so he can concentrate fully on the operation.

Haltor

Razor returned to Lassiter Island as instructed. He was feeling slightly nauseated at what he had just done.

Normally he didn't have a problem with killing. Those he killed in the past had been combatants, and he'd always tried to avoid killing innocents unless it had been absolutely necessary and there hadn't been any other way. He hadn't liked doing it but had rationalised it as a necessary evil, but this was just slaughter on a massive scale.

He was now a mass murderer.

He set down his ship on the landing pad as before and was shown to the Residence by the guards.

Lassiter was waiting for him when he arrived. This time, however, he was sitting out back on his veranda.

"It won't be long before the results of your work today hit the news media and spread all over the Coalition," he said as Razor walked onto the veranda.

"Come, take a seat, have a drink. Let's celebrate the success of the operation," he added.

Razor took the offered seat and tried to appear relaxed. The furniture was wicker with thick cushioned seats for comfort. A small glass-topped table sat between the chairs with a bottle of Scotch on a tray with another glass and a silver ice bucket. He reached forward, placed a handful of ice cubes into the tumbler, then poured a stiff measure of the amber liquid over them.

He needed a drink after what he had done to soften the feeling of disgust and dread.

"I'm impressed with your work today, Mister Razor. I almost thought you wouldn't go through with it," Lassiter said.

"I wasn't given much choice, Mister Lassiter," Razor replied. He was feeling more relaxed and confident after he felt the whisky start to warm through him.

"No, you weren't. That's true. You are an employee. I don't need your assurances. I just need you to do your job," Lassiter said.

"Well, I've done that, so am I done here? You said you had something more for me to do. Is that correct?"

"No, there is one other thing for you to do, at least for now."

Razor took another sip of his drink and then said, "What is it you want me to do?"

"I want you to make another delivery for me, but not yet. A message has to be delivered to the Coalition Council first."

"What do I do in the meantime?" Razor asked.

"Await further orders. Now finish your drink and piss off," Lassiter said.

Coalition Council HQ

President Parris had been informed of a contact having been made through the Emergency Comm Network.

He was rushed to the Situation Room, where a message was being made ready to play for the Council, and as leader, he had to be present.

As he entered the room, he saw the main monitor was alive with a haunting image of a shadowy figure against a back-drop of the dead world, Rideleus III.

"Ah, I see you've finally arrived, Mister President," the figure said, his or her voice passing through a series of filters to make it impossible to recognise.

"Yes, I'm here, and you have my full, undivided attention, sir. What is it you want from us, from me?" Parris replied.

"It's good that I have your attention because what I'm about to say is worth listening to," the shadow said with confidence.

"It's good that I have your attention because what I'm about to say is worth listening to," the shadow said with confidence.

"Go ahead, we're all listening," Parris urged. He knew this conversation in its entirety was being recorded so the tech analysts could go over it in minute detail to learn everything they could from it at a later date. For now, though, he had to listen to what this person had to say.

"I represent a small but extremely determined group called the Assembly for Criminal Enterprise, and our goal is to spread our reach across the galaxy. For us to reach this goal, we need funds, obviously, and to that end, we have a proposition for you. We are in possession of something you know a great deal about, the virus Omega Five. We acquired it from an associate of ours you may have heard of, Marcus Raine. We intend to sell this on the open market to the highest bidder. Now, we're not monsters. We understand that if the public learns of this transaction, there will be panic and chaos, which we will try to avoid. That's why you get the first choice. Pay our fee, and it will be handed over to you to do as you see fit. Refuse, and it goes to the highest bidder. With our contacts, I'm sure you wouldn't want any of them to get their hands on this.

"So, here we are. Do we have a deal or not?"

The room was silent as everyone absorbed what had been said.

Omega Five was still out there.

"Oh, I forgot to mention Rideleus III was our first test site. You know, to see if what we had was the real deal. Let me assure you it was. I mean, that place is a ghost town right about now; not a living soul survived. Not just people, though, I mean everything. If you ever want to visit a dead world, you have one right there," the shadow added.

That was the confirmation they had sought all along as to what caused the incident. This group was the cause, and they seemed totally indifferent to the effects they had caused on that world. To them, it was nothing more than a business transaction.

"How can we make a deal when you haven't told us what you want?" Parris said after clearing his throat to speak.

"How silly of me. Five billion Solar credits. I thought we'd start off small. Trust me, when those guys out there learn what we have and that it's for sale, the price will go through the roof. If you allow it to go to auction, I guarantee you will pay a lot higher than this one-time offer," the shadow replied.

"How long do I have to decide?" Parris asked.

"Until the end of this call, Mister President. The clock is ticking, sir."

"I have to confer with my council first. I can't just decide like that arbitrarily."

"You're the president. Of course, you can."

"You don't understand...."

The shadow cut him off with, "Ten..."

"What are you doing?"

"Nine..."

"This is preposterous."

"Eight..."

"Why are you doing this?"

"Seven..."

"You're insane."

"Six..."

"I can't just make a decision like that."

"Five..."

Parris was looking around the table for help, guidance, anything.

"Four..."

The countdown continued, and he was helpless.

"Three..."

What could he do, allow it to slip through his fingers or take the chance they caught this group before Omega Five went on sale?

"Two…"

"Okay, okay, you win. I accept," he said finally, his shoulders sagging in defeat.

"I'll be in touch with how and when to pay."

The call was ended abruptly.

Parris stood up straight, all visible signs of tension melting away as he looked at the screen. "Did I keep him talking long enough for you to run a trace on the call?" he asked.

The screen came back to life as the shadow returned.

"Don't bother to try and track this call. I made sure it was routed through several layers of encryption and bypassed through multiple layers of servers around several star systems.

"I do have one final demand to make. When the payment is made, I want a certain individual to make the delivery in person. You'll know who I mean. He was responsible for the destruction of a Dust manufacturing plant on Praxis. I want him present to personally make the transfer when the time is right. This is non-negotiable.

"Have a good day, gentlemen and ladies," the shadow said, then once more ended the call.

Parris turned to the rest of the room and, without a word, stormed out.

He had a call to make.

Chapter 24

SecOps HQ

"From what I can see, you're fully fit for active duty," Doctor Anderson said after giving Duncan a thorough examination.

"Thanks, Doc," he replied. He was relieved to hear that bit of news. Suspecting as much, it was still a relief to hear it.

He left the Med Lab and headed back to C's office.

As he entered, he saw C's face was dark and troubled and knew something had happened in his brief time at the Med Lab. Things had ramped up more, and they were entering the enemy's endgame.

"I see you've finally been cleared for active duty," he said, looking up at Duncan.

"Yes, sir. Glad to get back to work, officially," he replied.

"In that case, we'd best get to it then. I've just had a call from President Parris. He received a call from someone claiming responsibility for the attack on Rideleus III. They claim to have a supply of Omega Five and are willing to put it on the open market if the president doesn't pay five billion Solar credits. There's more, they want you present to make the transfer of funds. It seems they want the person who destroyed their Dust manufacturing facility on Praxis."

"So, this has been their plan all along. To get me?" Duncan asked. "No, it can't be that simple. Why go to all that trouble to get to me when there are so many other ways much easier?" he said.

"Isn't that being just a little narcissistic of you to consider it all being about you?"

"I agree, sir, and that's why I don't think it is. I think this is what it appears to be, and the chance to get to me is simply a bonus on their part."

"That's my assumption also."

"What have we got to go on, sir?" he asked.

"We went over the list that La Roche gave us, and we deduced that he was right; they had covered their tracks amazingly well."

"How does that help us, sir?" Duncan asked, confusion narrowing his brow.

"It helps us because although they left no tracks to follow, the information on the hits could only come from a protected source."

Duncan jumped on this straight away, "You have an idea who that source is, don't you, sir," he said.

Smiling briefly, C said, "I have an idea, yes."

"I'm guessing the government," Duncan said.

"And you'd be right, which is why we have to tread extremely carefully with this. If it's who I think it is, then they are connected at the highest level," C said.

"Are you suggesting someone in the president's staff, sir?" Duncan asked incredulously.

"I'm afraid so. It seems corruption is never far from the halls of power."

"What can we do, sir?" Duncan asked, ready to go to work.

"First, we need to see if my suspicions are correct."

"How do you intend on doing that, sir?" Duncan asked.

"The simplest method is just to ask them. I've asked to meet with the committee who were investigating the incident on Haltor."

"I thought you said they had been told it had been called off."

"It has, so this meeting will intrigue them, especially as I told them I had some new information for them."

"What information, sir?"

"I want you there with me. I want to see their expression when they see you. The person behind this will recognise you, I'm sure of it, while the rest won't have a clue who you are. You see, the entire investigation was to learn your identity and who you worked for. I now believe they had some information about you, but they just needed it confirmed so they could take you and the Ministry down in one action."

"Are you sure about this, sir?" Duncan asked.

"All their attempts at killing you have so far failed. This last move to get you to be the one to make the transfer in person is their last-ditch effort to get to you. They probably realise they lost their chance at this organisation but have one last chance at getting to you."

"You think they intend on killing me once the transfer is completed."

"Why else would they insist on you being present? It was made clear they wanted the person responsible for the destruction of their Dust manufacturing facility. Claiming responsibility in that way answers two questions that have been bothering us, who owned the facility and who was behind the recent events. They are the same people."

"Knowing it doesn't help us bring them down, though, sir. This plan of theirs seems to give them everything they want, money for the virus, my death, and their continued anonymity. Once we give them what they want, there's no guarantee they won't keep some of the Omega Five back or retain the ability to manufacture more. We have to put an end to this once and for all. We have to shut them down."

"I agree, but how?" C asked.

"I have an idea, sir, but it's a long shot," Duncan said.

Chapter 25

Coalition Council HQ

The wait had been interminable. The transfer of funds had been authorised, and now the entire room was waiting for the last details so this nightmare could end.

No one had left the room all night, and as the sun rose on a new day, the tension in the room was as palpable as the body odour coming from all the unwashed bodies present.

President Parris sat in his chair, drumming his fingers nervously on the tabletop as he stared at the blank screen.

"I now know what they mean when they say a watched pot never boils," he muttered to himself.

"Excuse me, sir?" his chief of staff asked.

Parris waved him off as the screen came alive, and a new call was put through. The same shadowy image was shown as before, and the same altered voice began speaking.

"Good morning, gentlemen. I hope you all slept well and that you've put everything in place," it said.

"Get on with it," Parris snapped. He disliked being held to ransom like this.

"Down to business, it is then. The person who will make the transfer will come alone to Haltor, where he will be met. He will make the transfer of funds, and then we will arrange for the Omega Five sample to be returned to you."

"That's not acceptable. You said that if we transferred the funds, you would return the Omega Five to us. It was implied that it would be a straight transfer—the funds for the bioweapon. We have kept to the demands you made. Now show us you can be trusted and transfer the bioweapon when the funds are transferred," Parris said, taking a huge gamble.

A slight pause followed while the president thought he'd pushed too hard.

"You are in no position to bargain," the shadow said, pausing before continuing, "but in this instance, I will allow it. The sample will be transferred the moment the funds have been confirmed. The transfer will take place in one hour. The exact location has been downloaded to your server," the shadow said, and the call ended.

Parris said, "Okay, the game is on."

"Haltor, one hour. The exact coordinates have been sent to your PIN," C said.

Duncan was sitting in the command chair of his ship, waiting for the call.

"Copy that, sir. I'm on my way," Duncan replied, and the ship's AI started the engines, having listened in on the conversation.

"The jump to Haltor has been laid in, sir, and the jump is ready on your command," the AI said.

The ship lifted off and shot into the air and was soon travelling through the upper atmosphere. As the light faded away behind the ship and the darkness of space shrouded the ship in its inky folds, Duncan was ready to make the jump.

"Okay, Ship, make the jump," he said.

The hyperspace window opened, and the small sleek craft flew through, emerging close to the planet Haltor.

"You have the coordinates, Ship. Take me down as close to them as possible. Run sensor scans on the way down. Usual protocols apply here, Ship. I want to know what I'm heading into here," Duncan said. As the AI prepared for landing, Duncan left the command chair and went into the rear compartment to check out his equipment.

The coordinates were in a secluded area away from any city. An ideal location for a trap. Once he was on the ground, he would be isolated. No one could sneak up on him, but also, conversely, anyone coming could see if he had any backup nearby.

Razor was waiting for the delivery man to arrive. He had his team located nearby, and they were all armed and placed where no one would suspect or, better than that, could see them.

It was a perfect setup that Lassiter had devised for them.

"The delivery man will be arriving in the next few minutes. Check your weapons and stand ready to move," Razor said through his comms.

The comms blipped to inform him that they were all ready.

Duncan was prepared as the ship came in to land. The landing area had been cleared, and the sensor scans had picked up nothing.

"Where the fuck are they? I can't imagine no one is waiting for me," he said. "Ship, run another scan of the immediate area. They have to be here somewhere. See if you can detect any shielding they could be hiding behind."

"Copy that, sir," the AI replied.

The ship put down, landing thrusters firing, kicking up dirt as the landing struts touched down.

Duncan was dressed in a tee shirt, cargo pants, and a thin jacket, under which he wore a shoulder holster with his SAP10 inside.

Opening the hatch, he walked down the ramp, leaving his ship behind. "Any sign of shielding?" he asked through his comms.

"There are several life signs suddenly appearing on my scopes, sir," the AI replied, alerting him to what he expected.

"Do not move," a voice ordered from behind him.

"Here we go," Duncan said quietly as he turned slowly to see a group of armed men moving to surround him.

Chapter 26

Duncan stood his ground and waited to see what would happen. With at least six people all standing around holding pistols on him, he knew he had no chance of escape if they decided to open fire.

"I'm here. Shall we get on with the transfer?" he suggested. He recognised Razor the moment he stepped forward and instinctively knew he would be the leader of this team.

"Have you authorisation to make the transfer?" Razor asked.

"That's one of the reasons I'm here," Duncan replied.

Razor held out a data transfer module. "This module is connected to the holding server the credits are to be transferred into. Make the transfer now," he said.

"Where's the Omega Five sample?" Duncan asked. "I'm not transferring anything until I know the sample is here," he said, unmoving.

Razor smiled, "Go, bring it out," he said to one of his team.

The man returned holding a small case, and he stood behind Razor.

"You'll forgive me if I don't open it. We don't want any slip-ups, now do we?" Razor said with a confident smile.

Duncan stepped forward and held out his PIN. He input a signal and then looked at the man in front of him. "The transfer is complete. I'll take the sample now and be on my way back," he said.

Razor checked the transfer and said, "Thank you for that, but you'll not be leaving. I'm afraid my boss has other plans for you. You're coming with us."

He signalled his team to move in.

Duncan was ready for this. He'd more than merely expected it; he'd hoped for it. It had been part of his plan. What he hadn't planned on was what came next.

Pain exploded across his entire body, centred on the small of his back. All his muscles tightened, and he went stiff as a board, unable to move.

His anguished brain immediately remembered his recent torture, and panic gripped him as tightly as his inert muscles had, but he was unable to do anything about it. He lost control of his emotions as terror rose up within him like a tsunami, and he realised he was helpless.

His last thought before darkness mercifully gripped him was that he had failed, and then everything went black.

SecOps HQ

"What just happened?" C asked. He was in the Situation Room along with the staff monitoring the operation.

"His vitals went through the roof, sir, just before they stabilised," Doctor Willetts said. He was on hand to monitor Duncan's vital signs considering what he had just been through.

"Why is that? What just happened?" C wanted to know.

"Something drastic."

"Such as, Doc? You'll have to be more specific," C said.

"I would say he was hit with a stun weapon of some sort, possibly electrical, but don't quote me. I'm just a doctor, not a weapons specialist," Willetts replied.

"Okay then, Doctor. As a physician, what can you tell me about Agent Pryde? Let's be specific. Is he able to continue with the operation?" C asked.

"Without having him here in front of me, I can't answer that. I'm sorry, sir. That's all I can tell you," Willetts replied apologetically.

Turning from the screen, C quietly said, "I just hope I haven't sent you in too soon."

Haltor

Duncan opened his eyes, and pain hit him right in the head. Excruciating, agonising pain stabbed him in both eyes as the light seemed to explode in front of him.

He closed them as quickly as he could and kept them tightly closed, trying to force the light out and reduce the pain.

It was soon obvious he was shackled because he couldn't move his arms or legs. He was spread eagle, arms out wide and legs splayed, so he knew he was in trouble. Gaining control of his emotions, he dampened down his anxiety and fear and calmed his breathing. After the initial shock of waking up in his present situation, he felt his heart rate slowing, and he was once more under control. Now he had to figure out where he was and what they intended to do to him.

The light was getting dimmer, but he wasn't sure if it was because he was getting used to the intensity or if it was actually reducing intensity. Either way, he was thankful for the reduction in pain. Slowly, he opened his eyes again, and this time he could see.

He was in a large room with a low ceiling that resembled a bunker of some kind. The walls were bare, with strip lights hung across the ceiling, giving off the only illumination. Directly in front of him was a stand that held a large round light bulb which was turned off. Clearly, this had been the source of his discomfort, but what purpose did it have other than the obvious one, he wondered.

"Okay, you're awake finally. Good, now we can continue with why you're here," a voice said. Coming into view was a tall man dressed elegantly in a suit that Duncan noticed probably cost more than half his yearly salary.

"I take it you didn't return the sample of Omega Five?" Duncan said, already knowing the answer.

"That was never my intention."

"Then I take it I'm in the presence of the man in charge," Duncan said.

"You are, indeed. I am the bad guy, which makes you the good guy, except that in this story, the bad guy wins."

Duncan looked at the man and, frowning, said, "I'm sorry, and I know this might sound strange. I feel I should know who you are, but I honestly don't have a clue."

With a sneer of contempt, he said, "It's not important, but I shall introduce myself nonetheless. I am William Lassiter."

"What do you intend on doing with the sample?" Duncan asked. He wanted to keep him talking to learn as much as he could while he tried to formulate a plan of escape.

"What I always intended on doing with it. Sell it, of course, along with more of it."

"More of it?" Duncan asked incredulously.

"Once you have a sample, it's quite easy to replicate," Lassiter told him.

"But that's insane. Why would you do that?" Duncan asked.

"To make money, isn't that obvious? Money is power, and while I have this bioweapon, I hold the ultimate power. People will pay whatever price I place on it just to have it."

"I'm finding it difficult to understand your motivation here, Lassiter. Omega Five can strip a planet of all life, so why would you want to sell that kind of power on the open market?" Duncan asked, looking at it logically.

Lassiter leaned in a little closer and said, "I have a fortune that I couldn't possibly spend in many lifetimes. I can do whatever I want and go anywhere I want; there are no obstacles having this kind of wealth cannot overcome, so why would I be concerned about what others might do with Omega Five? It doesn't concern me in the slightest."

"I see it now. You're insane," Duncan said plainly.

Lassiter angrily slapped him across the face. "Don't presume to think you know me; you don't," he said.

"Answer me this then. Why am I here?" Duncan asked, changing tack.

"You are the agent responsible for the destruction of my Dust facility. This is merely retribution," Lassiter replied.

"I take it you have something grand planned for me, or do you intend on making me talk about who I work for?"

"I don't care who you work for. It doesn't matter. They cannot stop me anyway. No, I'm not interested in you or any of that. You're here because I want to see you die. As soon as my present operation is complete, I will get around to dealing with you."

Lassiter turned to leave, then with a broad smile, said, "Don't go far."

"Funny, you think you're funny," Duncan commented to his back as he left.

Chapter 27

Sanchez Jumped from the hatch in the CSS Apollo, which had followed Duncan. She was wearing an orbital jumpsuit, a cross between an EVA suit and a HALO jumpsuit.

She hit the atmosphere at terminal velocity and felt friction from her passing through the air, heating her up. The cooling coils inside the suit reduced the heat and kept her from boiling up.

She kept her arms and legs close to her body as she flew down toward the ground. The altimeter on her Heads-Up Display in her helmet counted down the distance to the ground. When the counter read ten thousand feet, she opened her arms and legs out to the arch position for better control.

Wind rustled past her as she continued her descent to the ground. She operated the parachute and felt the drag as the canopy billowed out above her, filling to slow her descent.

She'd timed her jump so that she would reach the location where they had taken Duncan. As she homed in on it, she steered herself closer to a landing spot on the target area, Lassiter Island.

The ground came rushing toward her at an alarming rate. She braced herself for the impact and, in seconds, was touching down, bending at the knees to absorb the impact.

Stripping out of her harness, allowing the parachute to be dragged back into the pack, she continued toward her target.

Landing on the edge of the estate, she travelled toward the villa in the centre.

She just hoped she had arrived in time.

Duncan was beginning to ache from being shackled against the wall when the door burst open, and Lassiter stormed in.

"You think you're smart, don't you," he said, striding up to stand right in front of him, staring accusingly and wide-eyed at him.

"Did something happen?" Duncan asked with a straight face.

"You know full well what has happened. You implanted a trojan horse into the transfer of funds that attacked my account. It transferred all of my money to an unknown location. My account has been emptied."

"I have no idea what you're talking about. I'm just the delivery man, nothing more," Duncan told him calmly.

"Well, you just made the worst mistake in the history of mistakes. I'm going to use the Omega Five to wipe out your home planet and that of the Coalition homeworld before I move on to the rest of the colonies. You think you can mess with me; I'll make you all live to regret it," Lassiter ranted in front of him, spittle flying from his mouth as he was in danger of losing control.

"You'll find that difficult with just the sample," Duncan said.

"Did you honestly think I didn't have the ability to replicate more of the Omega Five virus? I have enough to destroy more than all the planets in the known galaxy," Lassiter shouted. "And now you're all going to find out what true hell is like," he added, then turned and left the room. From outside the room, he heard him say, "Bring him along. I want him to see this."

Two guards entered the room. One stood back, holding a pulse rifle on him, while the other deactivated the shackles freeing him.

Duncan stepped forward from the wall, rubbing his arms to bring the circulation back into them.

"Don't do anything stupid," the guard holding the rifle said.

Duncan followed the first guard through the door as the remaining guard fell in step behind him.

Now that he was free from the room he'd been incarcerated in, it was time to make his move.

Stopping suddenly, the guard following closed the gap to dig the muzzle of his rifle into his back.

"Keep moving, jackass," he said, pushing the barrel deeper into his flesh.

Duncan spun around so fast he caught him unaware. He blocked the rifle away from his body with his right arm and delivered a knife-edge strike to his throat with his left. It was perfectly timed and executed. As the guard's hands reflexively went to his throat, he released his grip on the rifle. Duncan caught it before it fell to the floor and turned it on the guard in front. He fired a short, three-round burst into his back, killing him instantly before turning the weapon on the guard still clutching his throat and ending him, too.

He quickly relieved both bodies of their pistols and spare magazines once he knew they were dead.

Now he was free and armed. It was time to see what he could do to prevent Lassiter from unleashing hell on the galaxy.

Lassiter reached the main control centre of his underground base.

Lassiter glanced at the door when he thought he heard gunfire, and he realised the guards weren't behind him with the prisoner.

"Holy fuck!" he raged, "That bastard has escaped again," he said.

Razor was in the room with him. He'd been there waiting to see what was about to happen. He saw Lassiter's expression when he turned and didn't need it spelled out for him to know something bad had happened. When he heard the gunfire, he knew things were about to get worse still.

Lassiter turned to him, "Go, find that man. I'm finished with him. Kill him on sight," he said.

Razor left the room, pleased to finally have something to do.

Chapter 28

S anchez reached the closest perimeter to the villa just as alarms sounded around the building.

"Things are beginning to heat up in there," she said.

Touching her earbud and activating her comms channel, she said, "Sanchez to CSS Apollo, about to breach the perimeter, have the tac-team ready to drop on my mark."

"Copy that, standing by," came the swift reply.

Dressed in a black combat suit, she had a pulse rifle across her shoulders and a SAP10 strapped to her right thigh. On her belt was an assortment of grenades and magazines for her weapons.

Knowing time was running out, she breached the perimeter and entered the villa's grounds.

Now that he was out of his cell, he was free to roam. His first priority was to find where they stored the remainder of the Omega Five so he could destroy it.

The cell where he had been held was in a separate section of this labyrinthine facility, with much more he wasn't seeing. He realised it must have taken months to build, which meant Lassiter had planned this a long time ago.

This was not something that had been cobbled together quickly. It had taken careful planning and execution.

The basement area was vast, with tunnels leading to a variety of sections, and he knew it would take time to explore them all, time that he didn't have.

He used his PIN to see if he could gain access to any network in use in the villa or below. Most facilities of this nature had a computer network controlling systems such as life support or, in this case, the security protocols governing the biohazard inherent with this bioweapon. Once he had access, he brought up the schematics and floor plans.

It took some doing, but he found where they were keeping the Omega Five virus.

A pulse ran through his ear, telling him he was being hailed. Touching his earbud, he said, "Go ahead but make it fast."

"I'm heading toward the villa now. The strike team is on standby. What is your location?" Sanchez said in his ear.

"I'm heading toward the villa now. The strike team is on standby. What is your location?" Sanchez said in his ear.

"I'm in some sort of basement facility below the villa. They are manufacturing the virus; I'm heading toward it now to destroy it if possible. Have the Apollo ready a missile strike on this location using incendiary missiles in case I fail to destroy the Omega Five. We can't allow him to use this anywhere else," he replied.

"He has more of that stuff?" she said incredulously.

"That's what he told me, and he intends on using it across the galaxy on unsuspecting colonies. Forget about me, just order that strike," Duncan said and ended the call.

Cementing the location of the virus to memory, he set off to find it.

Sanchez was left with a decision she felt was impossible to make. Whether to leave Duncan to his fate and call in the strike or try to reach him and help him destroy the virus.

What should she do?

Duncan would do as he suggested she do. His mantra was, after all, the mission comes first. She wasn't like him, though. As logical as his order had been, it was hard to follow because she was always looking to save every life she could. Sacrificing one for the greater good was never something that sat well with her.

This was a situation different from any other she had faced before, though. She was on untrodden ground here and unsure how to make that first step.

It occurred to her then that she could do both.

Contacting the Apollo, she said, "Captain, I have reliable intel that there is a significant amount of the Omega Five virus somewhere in a facility beneath the villa I am about to breach. I want you to fire incendiary missiles at my location on my mark. I will lead you directly to the source. I cannot stress the importance of hitting this target, sir, and hit it with as many missiles as you have. It has to be completely destroyed. We cannot leave a single viable atom of that thing down there."

"Do I need to tell you if I do this, the chances of you surviving are zero?" the captain responded.

"I am aware of the risks involved, sir. This is more important than one life, though. I will give you the signal the moment I have the location, sir," she said.

"I'll be waiting for that signal with my finger on the button. Godspeed, Agent Sanchez," he replied, then ended the call.

Sanchez took a deep sigh.

"I always did want to go out with a bang," she said.

Razor reached the cell where they had been keeping the captive agent. He drew his pistol and strode in the direction he thought he might be heading.

He hadn't followed Lassiter into the control room, so it was safe to say he was going for the Omega Five sample to destroy it.

Checking the schematics on his PIN, he knew where he had to go. So far, he had been kept in the dark about certain details about the operation here. He was being paid handsomely, so he kept his opinions to himself. It still rankled with him having delivered the virus to Rideleus III. So many deaths were now on his head, which he was having trouble coming to terms with. He had plenty of blood on his hands, but this was different. These people were completely innocent of anything, and he had caused it.

The cell led to an array of tunnels that were like a maze. Now that he knew where the virus was being stored, he had better than a good idea of where the target was heading.

Chapter 29

The tunnels were empty, which was just as well. Duncan had little time to get to and destroy the Omega Five. If Lassiter wanted to complete his threat, then he had to get there and fast.

Concrete walls were well-lit by lights that ran along the ceiling. The middle of the tunnel was wide enough for a medium-sized vehicle to drive down.

Duncan ran down the centre of the tunnel, his SAP10 in his hand. The area he was looking for was just ahead. According to the schematics he'd memorised, it was just around the next corner.

As he reached it, he turned the corner and saw the section needed.

The room in front of him was seen through a glass wall with a door in the middle. Stretching out for at least the length of a football field, the room had containers lining both walls. Inside each container was Omega Five in liquid form, at least a hundred litres in each, more than enough to destroy every planet in the Coalition.

"Holy shit!" he said when he saw the enormity of it all.

Being so focussed on what was in front of him, Duncan never heard the approach from behind until it was almost too late.

The click of a slide injecting a round into a chamber alerted him at the very last second, and instinct took over. He fell to the ground, turning to face the attack as bullets struck the glass wall above his head.

Shards of glass showered him as the bullets destroyed the wall. Duncan returned fire, but his aim was off, and all he hit was air. His attacker had pressed his body against the wall of the corridor they were in.

Duncan rolled free around the corner of the corridor, hoping to use this as cover. He peered around it, firing at the assailant.

Catching only a glimpse of him, it took a second or two for him to identify his attacker. The recognition, when it hit him, was visceral and was like a shot to the gut.

His attacker was his torturer from not too long ago. Now was his chance to even the score.

This was an emotional response to a tense situation, one that he shouldn't have allowed to happen. Normally, he had his emotions under tighter control than this. He couldn't allow this man to affect his performance. Too much was at stake here for him to react in pure anger.

Taking a moment to address this, he went into a trance to quickly regain total control of himself. The burning rage he felt boiling up inside him had to be quelled. He covered it in a blanket to relieve the pain the memory brought with it. Pushing it down under this blanket, he subdued his inner turmoil, wrapping it inside this comforting control, and was finally able to relax.

When he opened his eyes, he knew what he must do.

He was on his feet and standing against the wall at the turn in the corridor, using that same wall as cover. Bullets ricocheted off the wall, sending bits of it flying out in a cloud of dust. Stepping out, he levelled his SAP10 at the figure down the corridor and was immediately tackled by him.

The impact took the both of them through the glass wall, destroying what was left of it as they landed on the floor inside the massive chamber where the virus was being stored.

Rolling around on the floor, covered in broken glass, Duncan found himself on the receiving end of a punch to the head. Stars danced before his eyes from the impact, but he quickly fought off another punch by blocking it with his forearms. Twisting and turning, he managed to dislodge his attacker from on top of him.

Rolling free in the opposite direction, Duncan was on his feet. Shaking the cobwebs from his mind, he looked his attacker in the eye.

"I'm not shackled like last time," he said. "Let's see how you fare when it's just you and me," he added.

"I like your confidence, but you overestimate your chances here," Razor countered. His comment didn't have the required effect, though, as Duncan kept his demeanour cool as ice. No emotion showed on his face at all.

"Enough talk," Duncan said as he faced off against his adversary. Both men were in fighting stances, balanced evenly on the balls of their feet, arms up, ready to cover, block or strike.

Razor was the first to move. Stepping forward, he burst into a flurry of punches followed by a roundhouse kick aimed at Duncan's head. Duncan defended by blocking each punch on his forearms then used a two-handed block to stop the kick.

Duncan countered with a roundhouse elbow strike immediately after blocking the kick. Razor was stunned by the blow, unbalanced because his right foot was still in the air, and he tumbled to the ground. He hit the floor as Duncan stepped back to give him space.

The floor was covered in broken glass, and as Razor stood up, he shook loose shards from him and looked at his adversary with renewed respect.

He came forward again, a little more caution in his strikes this time. He threw a right cross at Duncan's head, which he blocked on his left forearm, dropping his right arm to cover his ribs. Razor switched targets and threw a left fist at Duncan's head. Anticipating the switch, Duncan brought his left arm across to block the second punch, turning the move into a spinning back fist. The blow snapped Razor's head around so fast he almost fell back down to the floor again.

Taking a step back and shaking his head to clear it, Razor gave him a feral grin. He knew he had a fight on his hands here, but he relished the challenge.

Razor tried again to break through Duncan's defences, throwing a series of punches with the same effect as before. Duncan danced out of range of most until he saw an opening, which he took. Blocking a punch, he closed the gap, delivering another stunning elbow strike to the side of Razor's head, which sent him staggering back a few paces.

Duncan was in control, but he knew this had to end so that he could call in the strike on the island and destroy the virus.

Razor had similar thoughts about ending the struggle but for different reasons. Reaching behind his back, he pulled out a wicked-looking blade. It was nine inches long and double-edged, tapering to a point.

This added a new perspective to the fight now, a new level of danger for Duncan, as it changed the power dynamic in favour of Razor.

Stepping forward, he swung the blade sideways, thrusting it toward the stomach of his opponent. Duncan danced back with every swipe of the razor-sharp blade.

Duncan blocked another series of strikes aimed at his chest, turning the blade away from him every time, culminating in him grabbing the wrist that was holding the knife. Before he could slap the blade from Razor's hand, his attacker deftly changed hands, switching the knife from his right to left hand and then slashing Duncan across the arm.

Duncan released his hold and moved away as he felt the sharp pain from the cut. Blood oozed through his torn sleeve down his arm.

Seeing the blood boosted Razor's confidence, and he gave a little smile. He knew, the same as Duncan, that if he could inflict more damage like this, then the fight would sway in his favour.

This had to end now, Duncan knew.

Confining his emotions behind walls of mental concentration, Duncan fought on. Now was not the time to allow any emotion to seep through to his conscious mind. Now more than ever, he needed his ice-cold control.

Smiling, Razor came at him again, this time with more confidence. He was beginning to relish this conflict now as he saw he might be gaining the upper hand.

Stepping forward, he eyed Duncan warily, taunting him with dummy strikes before lunging at him again in earnest.

Duncan parried the lunge, grabbing Razor's wrist again, but this time he chopped the wrist, numbing the hand. The knife fell from his unfeeling fingers only to be caught by Duncan, who brought it up and buried it deep in Razor's throat.

Blood spurted from the wound. Razor's eyes went wide in surprise and horror. He never expected this outcome. Victory was literally snatched from his fingers.

Duncan moved the blade laterally across the throat, widening the wound and opening it up to hasten his opponent's demise.

Blood flowed swiftly as his heart pumped it through the opening. Razor's hands went up to his throat as Duncan yanked the blade free, removing the last obstacle and allowing more blood to escape. He watched Razor's eyes glaze over as blood loss ended his life, and he fell to his knees first before falling to his face, dead.

Duncan took a bio-patch from a pocket and slapped it over the wound on his arm. The nano-meds in the patch would seal his wound and apply broad antibiotics to fight off any infection, allowing him to continue.

Retrieving his weapon from the floor, he looked around to see what he could do to hasten the destruction of the Omega Five virus.

Chapter 30

Lassiter was monitoring the situation through sensors in and around the villa and sub-basement.

"If you need something done right, do it yourself," he said when he saw that Razor had failed. All the personnel who worked for him had trackers implanted in them. These trackers displayed all the subject's data to him on his screen. It showed bio-signs, location, and anything else he wanted that could be gleaned from it.

He saw Razor's signal go dark, which could only mean one thing. He was dead. Anger blazed inside him, centred on the man responsible. He knew he had to take care of him personally now before he did any more damage to his plan.

He reached for a sidearm from one of the guards and said, "Follow me," to two of them. He left the Situation Room and headed for the last place Razor was known to be alive, the storage room for the Omega Five virus.

Standing inside the room, looking at all the containers holding the virus, Duncan couldn't help but feel something.

He was standing in close proximity to enough of a substance that could wipe out all life across the galaxy. Even he felt daunted despite being in total control of his emotions. This was just too vast not to be affected by it.

He touched his earbud and said, "Sanchez, this is bigger than we thought. I'm standing next to enough Omega Five to wipe out life across the galaxy. We need to call in the missile strike immediately."

"I'm on my way to you—eta ten minutes," Sanchez replied.

"Abort that and leave immediately. Get clear and call in the strike on my location. I will just have time to bail, but we must call in the strike now," he said more forcefully this time.

"Duncan, if I call it in now, you won't have time to get clear. You'll be caught up in the blast."

"I know the risks involved. It's more important to destroy this virus once and for all. If we wait any longer, there's a chance they'll have time to move it. Look, I'll do what I can to delay them from doing anything, but you have to call in that strike. Too many lives are at risk here. Just send in the strike."

He could almost hear his partner thinking about this, trying to come up with another solution where they all survived, but he was coming up empty.

Finally, she said, "Copy that. I'll give the Apollo the word. Duncan, good luck."

"Copy that," he said and signed off.

Once he had signed off, he started looking around for a way to help with the destruction of the containers. He had ordered a missile strike using incendiary warheads. Fire was always the best way to kill a virus, so he looked for a way to help along with that. If he could set a fire going down here, it would add to the effect the missiles would have.

Pipes ran along the walls at just over head height. These pipes helped distribute the cooling fluid to the containers to keep the virus in liquid form at a cool enough temperature to keep it stable. He would have to disconnect this first. The fluid used in the cooling pipes was flammable. All he had to do was divert some of the fluid into the room and set it alight. The fire would take care of the rest. Not only did they have to destroy this supply of the virus, but they had to ensure that their ability to manufacture more of it was destroyed, too.

He set about uncoupling one of the pipes at one of the joints, and the cooling fluid started to pour through.

He stepped back and watched it land on the floor for a second before he would ignite it. Once he was sure it was burning, he would find a way out.

As he waited for enough of the fluid to pool on the floor, he heard something outside the room.

"There he is. Kill him," a voice ordered from outside the room. He recognised it as Lassiter's voice. He'd arrived with two more armed guards, and they were about to open fire on him.

Lassiter led the guards around the corner and saw the shattered glass walls of the container section.

"There he is, kill him," he shouted, and the guards opened fire.

A bullet struck the wall and ricocheted off onto one of the containers in a shower of sparks.

"Wait, be careful. If you puncture one of those containers, we are all dead, as well as everyone else on this planet," Lassiter shouted at the guards. They immediately ceased firing, staring at him.

Duncan had ducked into a recess in the wall between two of the containers. He held his breath until the shooting stopped. The second it did, he stepped out and returned fire. His first salvo hit one of the guards, knocking him off his feet as the bullets hit him in the chest. The large calibre bullets had enough force to punch a hole in the target large enough to put your fist through.

Duncan came running toward the wall, firing as he went, forcing the other two to back off. He dove through the shattered walls and twisted in mid-air, firing behind him into the pool of cooling fluid on the floor. The bullet struck the floor, sending up sparks that ignited the liquid.

The fluid ignited in a powerful explosion that soon spread across the floor and up the containers.

As Duncan hit the floor outside the room, he could already feel the heat from the flames behind him.

Time to leave.

Lassiter saw his plans literally go up in smoke as the room caught fire.

He was so incensed by this that he started firing at Duncan, the focus of all his rage and frustration. He kept on firing until the clip was empty. He was so enraged that he didn't care if the bullets hit their mark or not, which none of them did.

Still, he fired even when Duncan dove through the wall landing close to his feet. The bullets missed their mark as rage made his hands shake.

Duncan dealt with the remaining guard first, shooting him in the head as he approached Lassiter. He saw the latter's eyes go wide as he noticed the fire beginning to build in his precious containment room.

Duncan was close to him by this time. Lassiter aimed once more and fired one last time. Duncan felt the impact on his upper body as the bullet hit him. It spun him around, knocking him off balance, and he fell to the floor face-first. He saw the blood flowing from a hole in his chest. Pain would come later when the shock of being shot had closed off enough of his senses for his body to cope with the fact. He had to act fast before it incapacitated him. Taking out another bio-patch, he slapped it over the wound directly on his skin and waited a moment for the meds to kick in. The patch would stem the blood flow, sealing the wound, but with the bullet still inside him, there was only so much the patch could accomplish. For him to make a full recovery, it had to be removed, but that could be dealt with later. Right now, he had greater things to attend to.

Chapter 31

Lassiter ran off the instant he realised there was no saving his supply of the Omega Five. His plan had been thwarted once again by this lone operator, and he was furious.

As he left the area, he came up with a plan. He would have his revenge. They may have rid him of his fortune, and they may have destroyed his supply of the greatest weapon ever, but not all of it. He would show them all that he was someone not to be trifled with.

He reached an express elevator and pressed the control to take him topside. There was a landing pad nearby which housed a small craft. He ran over to it and boarded through a ramp on the side. His access led to the flight section in the forward area of the craft.

"Prepare for immediate take-off," he said, and the AI started the engines. The thrusters lifted the ship into the air, and then the main engines fired, sending the craft speeding into the upper atmosphere.

"Set course for Terra II," he said.

"Course laid in," the AI replied.

"Make the jump," Lassiter ordered.

Duncan reached the elevator and entered as the missiles were fired from the Apollo in orbit.

The missiles had targeted the villa on Lassiter Island and passed through the upper atmosphere just as Lassiter was taking off.

Duncan reached the ground level inside the villa as a call came through.

"The missiles are on the way, eta twenty seconds," Sanchez informed him.

As soon as he heard that, he knew his time had run out.

"Lassiter has escaped. I fear he may have some of the Omega Five virus on board," he said as he ran for his ship.

"I'll have the Apollo track him if they can't stop him, but you need to get out of there now," Sanchez said urgently.

"Ship, I need an exfil within the next twenty seconds," he said, communicating with his ship.

"Copy that, Commander. I am on my way," replied his ship's AI.

He ran as fast as he could. Personnel from down below had no idea what was about to happen, and neither did the staff in the villa. The sight of both Lassiter and a stranger running to leave the villa sent a wave of confusion and panic through them, and they, too, decided to follow.

The sound of the approaching missiles filled the air like a horde of banshees.

Duncan reached the perimeter of the villa's grounds as the first missile hit. The explosion sent a massive fireball into the air, followed by more as each successive missile hit.

The entire villa was destroyed, and as the fireballs engulfed the sprawling basement, more of the ground fell as the explosions imploded this cavern.

Duncan ran for his life as the ground collapsed behind him. The ship swooped in low, trying to reach him before he fell into the opening behind him.

"Commander, I suggest you jump for the ramp before it is too late," the AI said in his ear.

Taking the advice, Duncan leaped into the air as the ship neared his position. The ground opened up below him, and the heat from the flames hit him like a furnace. His hand landed on the ramp and took hold. The ship lifted higher into the air, taking him from the fire below. As the ship went higher, Duncan felt his arm stretch. His shoulder popped with the strain, almost dislocating by the pull of gravity.

He let out a groan as the pain from his shoulder flooded his brain. He reached up with his other arm to take the strain off his sore arm. Using the remainder of his rapidly waning strength, he pulled himself up level with the ramp's edge. Throwing his right leg up onto it, he used his heel to dig in and leverage himself over the edge and onto the ramp.

As he rolled over, he lay there to regain his breath for a second or two before getting to his feet.

"Ship, do you have the whereabouts of Lassiter and the remaining sample of Omega Five?" he said as he made his way toward the flight deck of his ship.

"A ship departing your last location was seen leaving the area through a hyperspace window," the AI replied.

"Any thoughts on where he might be going?" he asked. Before his ship could respond, he said, "Never mind, I know exactly where he's going. Set course for Terra II and make the jump."

Chapter 32

Terra II

Lassiter looked at the planet below, taking in the blue orb that was the second home of the human race. Blue oceans covered in a thin patina of clouds that resembled balls of cotton wool sat side by side with green land masses. Even from his vantage point high above the planet, he could make out the vast city complexes that covered huge areas of the ground.

All of this was about to be wiped out. This would be his revenge for the interference of the Coalition in his plans to dominate the galaxy. They would not live long enough to regret it, at least not those on the planet below.

The news of what he was about to do would soon spread to the other colonies. What they learned would speed up their search for him.

He had contingencies for that, as he had for everything.

"Take me down," he said, and the ship entered the atmosphere heading for the ground.

Duncan saw the ship headed toward the ground. There were others in orbit, coming and going from one of the busiest planets with the most populace shipping lanes in the galaxy. Duncan recognised the one he needed and followed it as soon as he re-entered normal space.

"Ship, contact HQ, and give them a sit-rep. Let them know I'm going after Lassiter and tell them they need to take precautions should I fail to stop him. I would suggest the same incendiary missile strike be made ready for launch," he said.

"Copy that, sir," the AI replied.

Duncan knew he couldn't be distracted by anything at the moment. He needed to focus all his attention on the task at hand. He had to stop Lassiter before he let loose the Omega Five on his home world.

Sanchez arrived back at Terra II aboard the Apollo.

"Sir, we just arrived back in orbit. The threat on Haltor has been destroyed," she said through the comm link.

"Duncan has followed Lassiter here and is trailing him in the hope of stopping him before he uses the sample of Omega Five he has with him," Chambers replied.

"Holy shit, I thought we finished that threat off on Haltor," Sanchez commented. "What do you want me to do, sir?" she asked.

"He has ordered a missile strike in case he fails to stop Lassiter from deploying the virus. He's asked for the missiles to have incendiary warheads deployed."

"Makes sense, sir. It's how we destroyed it on Haltor. Send me the coordinates of Duncan's location, and I'll be his backup."

"Already sent. Good luck, Agent Sanchez."

Sanchez left her quarters and went directly to the hold where her ship was in dock.

As she boarded and took her seat, she contacted the captain to inform him of her intentions. Seconds later, she exited the Apollo and was headed toward the planet's surface.

Lassiter landed at a private spaceport owned by his corporation. He had business interests across the galaxy, so finding somewhere to put down wasn't a problem.

The spaceport was in a remote area of New London outside the city limits. He exited his ship and transferred the container holding the Omega Five into the trunk of a vehicle he had the use of that was left for him.

He got behind the wheel and started the engine. Settled in, he set the navigation controls to the coordinates he wanted and set off, selecting the self-drive mode. He sat back to enjoy the ride.

Duncan saw where the ship had landed and instructed the ship's AI to get as near as possible and set down there.

By the time he landed, the entire spaceport was empty. The ship Lassiter had used to escape was still where it had been left.

"Where the hell are you now?" he said when he saw there was no sight of him.

"Where the hell are you going?" he asked the question most prevalent in his mind.

Approaching the problem logically, he knew if he was going to use the virus, he could drop it anywhere on the planet to achieve the same result. It did not matter in the slightest where he distributed it. The result would be the same, total destruction of all life on the planet. So, what was he doing? What was his plan?

Trying to get inside his mind, he put himself in his shoes, trying to experience what had happened from Lassiter's perspective.

He had planned on destroying as many planets in the galaxy as he could. That had been prevented. What would he want, retribution for the interference in his plans? How would he achieve that goal? How would he go about punishing those who interfered?

Punishment—that was the key here. How would he do that? What would be the best way to punish his enemy?

The realisation hit him like the shock of a cold shower. It almost took his breath away.

He knew exactly what he was going to do, and in that moment, knew exactly where to find him.

He rushed back into his ship to get his bike; he would need the most mobile and swiftest of transports if he wanted to reach Lassiter before he accomplished his plan. Riding his bike down the ramp at the back of his ship, he set off after Lassiter, and he just hoped he would get there in time.

Chapter 33

As soon as Duncan arrived in the city, he realised the enormity of the task he'd set himself. Although it was entirely logical Lassiter would attack this city where the heart of the Coalition Council resided, finding him within a population of over twenty million people was an impossible task. Given that he could lash out with the virus at any time, he was definitely working against the clock and needed more than a little help.

He rode directly to the SecOps HQ, where he went to see Chambers.

"We need to use every sensor available to us to locate Lassiter, and we need to do it fast," he said as he entered the Situation Room.

"I take it you lost him," Chambers replied. He was standing, staring at the wall-mounted monitor screen, which displayed various scenes around the city. "I've already initiated a series of scans around the city, but it's like looking for a needle in a stack of needles."

"We have to narrow it down somehow," Duncan said urgently.

"I know, I have teams trying to do just that."

"What results have you come up with so far?"

"Not enough, I'm afraid."

"There must be something we can do," Duncan said. "Where would he go to do the most harm, do you think? He would need an exfil as well, I can't think he would go to all this trouble to not enjoy the results. He's not the type to sacrifice himself just to get what he wants; it goes against everything we know about the man."

"If he wants to inflict maximum damage and wants to punish us here, then he would detonate an explosive device in the heart of this city while he remains able to leave the planet," Chambers posited.

"How would you go about that if you were him?" Duncan asked. He was finding it difficult to think straight as the stress of recent events was building up inside him despite his endeavours to dampen down on all his emotions.

"The simplest method would be to weaponise the virus and fire a missile with a warhead containing the bioweapon from a remote location, or even from orbit."

"I agree. We need to look into all the properties Lassiter owns in and around the city. It has to be somewhere large enough for him to launch a missile from," Duncan suggested.

"Why not from orbit? Surely, that would be the best option. It would speed up his exit from the scene?" Chambers asked.

"He would have to assume that we would be scanning for craft in orbit and take measures to stop them. I think he's somewhere close by, preparing to deliver his killing blow to this entire planet," Duncan said.

Chambers nodded and signalled to one of his aides to change the parameters of their search to incorporate this new data.

On the main viewer, a series of new images appeared on all of the properties, all of them large and luxurious.

"We have the list of Lassiter's properties up on the screen, sir," the aide said.

"Yes, I can see that. Good work. I want teams sent to each location immediately, ready to strike," Chambers ordered.

Duncan said, "I'll take the coastal one. An island would be a good place to house a launch pad. As soon as I have confirmation, I would suggest you prepare a missile strike just to be sure."

"I'll send Agent Sanchez to your location as backup," Chambers said.

With that, Duncan left the room to return to his ship.

He had work to do. This was not over, not until he had stopped Lassiter, once and for all.

Lassiter left the city and was soon reaching the coastal area where he had a residence on an island he had purchased. His need for isolation and privacy meant this was his ideal choice and was his favourite place on the planet among all the others he owned.

The other places he had were mainly for business purposes or at least matters that pertained to his many business interests. His island was a home from home.

It was situated five miles off the coast, with the only access by boat or small aircraft. The island was small, covering a mere three square miles, but it was adequate for his needs.

A boat was moored at the dock, and he drove onto it. Once he had secured the vehicle, he went into the pilot house and fired up the engine, a caterpillar drive. The magnetohydrodynamic drive, or MHD, pulled water into the thrust chambers and pushed it through to exit at the rear, forming an effortless propulsion. The speed picked up, and he was soon travelling across the water, reaching speeds of close to eighty knots.

The island was in sight, and he was soon pulling up to the pier, where his dock hands helped secure the boat upon his arrival.

He drove his vehicle off the boat up to his residence on the edge of a cliff overlooking the sea around the island.

He retained a small staff on the island so that it was always ready for his arrival, just as it was today. He had the security staff transport the cargo from the trunk of the vehicle to the basement of his residence.

When he reached there, he looked around at the space he had built. He felt satisfaction. He finally could see the future clearly and knew what he must do to bring the Coalition to its knees.

Chapter 34

As he approached the coastal area where Lassiter had his island, Duncan scanned the area for weapons and any sign of containment fields he may have in place for biohazards.

"I can see no signs of bio-containment protocols in place in or around the island residence, Commander," the AI informed him.

"He may not have had time to put any in place, especially if he never intended bringing the Omega Five here in the first place," Duncan said.

"That would make sense, sir. Are you suggesting that this is a tangential addition to his plan, an offshoot as it were?"

"Exactly that, Ship. He's now playing things by ear. He's making it up as he goes along, which could make things more dangerous than ever. He's more likely to make decisions on pure emotion rather than thinking them through to a logical conclusion," Duncan said, expressing his worst fear about the situation.

"Understood, sir. What are your intentions, and what do you need of me?" the AI asked. It was programmed to work as a partner when none was available. It had autonomous control over the ship and its weaponry and would protect the operator it had been assigned to.

"I need to get across to that island without being spotted. It's best I go underwater and attempt ingress at an unpopulated area, then work my way up to the building to see what he is doing," Duncan said.

"I have Agent Sanchez approaching, sir. She's on comms for you," the AI informed him.

"You arrived just at the right time," he said.

"I'm fine, thanks. Yes, I got away from the explosions safely; thanks for your concern," Sanchez replied sardonically.

"I plan on swimming across to the island underwater. I would make preparations to join me. I leave as soon as I am ready," he said, ignoring her earlier comments. He was totally focussed on the job at hand and wouldn't allow himself to be distracted by her flippant chatter.

"I'll be there in five," she replied. He could tell by her response that she, too, was aware of the time constraints on them both. She had obviously decided to put her emotions to one side to concentrate on the matter at hand.

Duncan was not thinking this. He was too busy getting ready for the next part of this mission. He stripped off his clothes and donned a wet suit with a hood. He wrapped a weight belt around his waist that also held certain weapons. He shrugged into a harness that held a holster for his SAP10 across his chest. Choosing a rebreather full-face mask, he placed it on his head and checked the airflow. When he was convinced everything worked as they should, he left the ship.

As he exited his own ship, he saw another coming in to land. It was Sanchez.

Dust was kicked up around him as the thrusters softened the descent of the arriving ship, and Duncan turned his head away to prevent it from getting covered in dirt.

"You look rough," Sanchez said as she left her ship. She held her rebreather under her arm, but she was wearing an outfit similar to Duncan's.

"I've had a few problems. I'm okay if that's what you're wondering," he replied, "how did you come to that conclusion? I'm wearing a full-face mask," he added.

"You forget that I know you probably better than most. I can tell by how you hold yourself and by your voice from our conversations," she replied.

"Okay, let's go, shall we?" he said.

"I'm all yours," she replied.

Duncan led the way to the water. He dove in and went under, immediately followed by Sanchez.

The water was cold, but the suit kept his core temperature close to normal. Visibility was good, at least a hundred metres or more. Fish of all species and varieties swam past his field of vision as he swam forward toward the island. He kept his depth to around twenty feet or so to minimise the threat of having to decompress coming up.

Sanchez swam up alongside him, keeping within visible range. No experienced diver ever went on a dive alone. Using that method reduced the threat of death if anything should happen when below the surface.

The swim took several minutes, and when they broke the surface, they were close to shore.

The night was closing in on them, which would help in the infiltration of the residence on the island and their plans to prevent the disaster Lassiter was no doubt planning.

Duncan emerged from the water slowly as he walked up the shoreline.

"Let's get to work," he said.

Chapter 35

"When will it be ready to launch?" Lassiter asked. He was standing, looking at the missile in his basement. It was a small rocket, no more than two feet in length, with the majority of that taken up by the propellant. The nose cone contained the cargo he had brought with him from Haltor.

The nose cone was the warhead, a weaponised version of the Omega Five virus, the last of his supply. The remainder of which had been destroyed in the attack on his island on Haltor.

He was about to claim his revenge by striking at the very heart of the organisation that had destroyed his plans, his organisation, and taken away his funds. All of which could be regained in time. He had done it once, so it was logical that he could do the same again.

"Are you serious about this?" asked his head of security, Carl Jacobs, who ran his security concerns on Terra II. He was ex-military and proud of his service. He was also just learning about the true nature of the man who employed him.

"Do I look like I'm joking to you?" Lassiter shot back angrily. He was getting frustrated at all the delays and just wanted this to get started so he could retreat to a safe distance and watch the outcome.

"That's what worries me, sir. You look completely calm and rational, but this is not the act of a rational man. If you do this, you are condemning millions of lives to death. Not only that, but you are destroying an entire planet's ecosystem. Terra II will be uninhabitable for years to come."

"What's your point, Jacobs?" Lassiter said calmly.

"I'm not sure I can be a party to this, sir. I cannot think of one reason why you would even consider something like this."

"They left me no choice, Jacobs. They meddled in my affairs, they pilfered my funds from the bank, they thwarted my plans, and now they attacked my very person. If I don't do this, who knows what they'll do to me," Lassiter said, his eyes growing wider the more he spoke.

Jacobs involuntarily took a few steps away from him when he saw this. His boss was quite mad, and he wasn't sure what to do next. He was torn between loyalty to the man who had provided so much for him during his employment and his need to warn the authorities about what he planned.

"Where are the controls for the missile?" Lassiter asked. Jacobs said nothing in return; he just glanced at the panel they were standing beside.

"Ah, good. You can go now, Jacobs. I can take it from here," he said, dismissing him with a wave of his hand.

Lassiter's fingers danced over the controls, inputting certain commands. Jacobs watched for a while before leaving, seeing the first set of commands.

Alone with the rocket on the launch pad, Lassiter set about the next phase of his hastily thought-out plan.

The house was not too far from the shore of the island. It seemed that Lassiter had a proclivity for his homes being near to water.

Duncan hand-signalled for Sanchez to follow him. He moved under cover of darkness from the shore to the walls at the base of the cliff. A staircase had been carved out of the rock face with a handrail built for safety opposite. The stairs led up the side of the cliff on which the villa was perched.

The higher he went, the more he struggled. His legs were burning from the strain, as were his lungs, but he dared not halt for fear he'd be too late. Sanchez followed him every step of the way, and he knew she would be faring much better than him. Perhaps it had been a mistake to come back to active duty so soon.

Doubt flooded his mind at that moment, and it took an enormous effort to control it. Once doubt enters the mind, it erodes the confidence, and once that happens, you make mistakes. Self-doubt, leading to a lack of confidence, is one of the hardest things to overcome. You can't just dismiss it, nor can you turn it off. It holds on tight, almost like a living thing strangling you slowly until you feel like you can do nothing.

Duncan wasn't like most people, though. He could control his emotions better than anyone on the planet, but even for him, this was a struggle. Closing his eyes as he took a breath, he gathered all his doubts together. Wrapping them inside a blanket of security, he placed them in a closed-off section of his mind. When he opened his eyes again, he was ready to continue once more.

He felt a hand on his shoulder, "You okay?" Sanchez asked softly, aware that any noise would travel far in this area.

"I'm fine," he replied in the same tone as he continued up the stairs.

When they finally reached the top, he peered over the edge to see what lay beyond. An armed guard was patrolling the perimeter of the villa's grounds. He wore a bored expression, feeling his duty was nothing but a waste of time. They were about to prove him wrong.

Duncan waited for the guard to pass him by, then sprang up over the edge and chased after him. Clamping a hand over his mouth to silence him, Duncan pushed his combat knife through the man's neck and then sliced forward, cutting through his oesophagus and silencing him permanently. Blood ran freely down the guard's shirt as he fell to the ground bleeding to death and unable to call for help. Duncan knew he would be dead in less than thirty seconds.

Sanchez followed him over the edge, and as soon as the guard had been neutralised, they made their way forward.

Keeping their heads down, they ran in a crouch toward the villa. When they reached the outside walls, Duncan flattened his back against it and turned to his partner.

"That was too easy. Something's not quite right here. There should be more guards. Security should be tighter," he said quietly.

"What do you want to do?" Sanchez asked.

"Our jobs," he replied without a moment's hesitation.

Chapter 36

After leaving Lassiter alone at the controls, Jacobs was in a quandary. Should he remain loyal to his employer, or should he contact the authorities about what he was about to do?

Knowing what he'd learned since Lassiter had arrived, it wasn't a difficult decision to make. Lassiter had gone off his mind; the man was insane. He was sure of that, and he had to be stopped. The rest of the world had to be warned, though, first.

He accessed a comm channel and called the local authority to inform them of the situation. The call was re-routed to the Coalition Council HQ, where President Parris took the call personally.

"This is President Parris. Go ahead and tell me what you know, sir," he said.

There was a pause for a second or two while Jacobs gathered his wits about him. He'd never expected to be talking to the president himself, so it came as a shock to learn he was on the other end of the call.

"I'm sorry, sir," he said to start with, then got right into it, "Lassiter is on his island and is readying to launch a missile at New London. This missile has a warhead loaded with something called Omega Five. He says it'll kill everything on the planet. Is that true, sir?"

"When is he going to launch, sir?" Parris asked, ignoring Jacob's question.

"In the next hour, I think, sir."

"Thank you, Mister Jacobs. I would suggest you leave that island as soon as possible, sir. We will handle everything from here, so don't you worry," Parris said and ended the call before Jacobs could ask more questions he didn't want to have to answer.

"Get me Director Chambers immediately, and clear the room," he said. An hour, Jacobs had said. That wasn't enough time to evacuate anyone, let alone all the inhabitants of this planet. A full evacuation would take months at least, which meant they had only one option, stop that missile from being launched.

When C came on the line, he said, "I've just had confirmation that Lassiter is on his island and is targeting New London with his missile loaded full of Omega Five. I'm going to order a full strike on his island, so if your man is there, I suggest you pull him out in ten minutes because, in ten minutes and one second, that island will cease to exist."

"Thank you for the warning, Mister President," C replied and signed off.

The Situation Room was already buzzing with tension. At the end of the call, a quiver of panic ran around it.

"Okay, people, let's not get excited here. Yes, the situation looks dire, but we have people on the ground who are more than capable of dealing with this. Worst case scenario, they don't get clear in time, but the missile strike will take out the Omega Five threat once and for all. Keep on working and let's all do our jobs," he said.

Moving to the back of the room where he wouldn't be overheard, he called Duncan.

"There's been a development here. We had confirmation of Lassiter's intentions; he has a warhead loaded with Omega Five on a missile aimed at New London. It's going to be launched within the next hour. You have 'til then to finish this and disarm that missile or be blown apart by the missiles aimed at you."

"So, no pressure then," Sanchez said as she had been linked to the call as well.

"Copy that, sir. We'll update you when the operation is complete," Duncan replied.

C knew Duncan wouldn't abandon his mission until he had done everything he could to complete it to success. He had never failed or given up on any mission for as long as he'd known him, and he couldn't see him starting now.

"Stay safe, you two, and hurry up and get off that island fast. I doubt I could call off that missile strike even if I wanted to," he said and ended the call.

As he walked back toward the rest of the room, Goodchild came to stand next to him.

"Everything alright, sir?" she asked.

"I've informed Duncan and Sanchez of the recent development. That's all I can do. It's up to them now," he said.

Chapter 37

"So, we're leaving, right? Letting the missiles take this place out, right?" Sanchez said, already knowing what Duncan would say.

"I'm staying. I have to finish this. I have to learn exactly who this Lassiter is. I have to know who is in charge of this group that's been after me since that incident on Praxis," Duncan replied honestly.

"None of that will be of any use to you if we both get blown to pieces," she argued.

"Then leave if you want to, but I'm staying," he said adamantly and pushed himself off the wall to head for the door.

"Holy shit, Duncan, if you get me killed here, I swear I'll haunt you for the rest of your damned life," she said before going after him.

He burst through the door; his arms extended as he peered down the sight of his SAP10, scanning left then right to clear any threats. He slowly went room to room, making sure it was safe to proceed. No one was at home. All the staff had left, and the only security guard they had come across had been dispatched outside.

"Where the fuck is everyone?" Sanchez said as she came up to him.

"I don't like this," Duncan said.

"Maybe they also heard about the missile strike coming their way and did what we should be doing and got the fuck out of here."

"You're being illogical," Duncan chided.

"The imminent threat of being blown up has that effect on me," she parried.

"Where would he keep the launch pad," Duncan said, ignoring his partner's ranting.

"We didn't come across anything like that on our way here," she said.

"Then it has to be down in the basement somewhere," he said.

Lassiter was about to enter the last commands into the control panel when he heard footsteps from somewhere above. Oh, they were trying their best to keep quiet, but since Jacobs had left him alone down there, the villa had gone unnaturally quiet, as if no one was at home.

He input a command and watched as the wall next to the rocket dropped down into the floor. The launcher swung out laterally through this opening to an area beyond the building where it could launch freely. As soon as the structure had locked into place, shields rose up around the rear end of the rocket so that when it launched, the flames from the propellant didn't start any fires.

Lassiter looked at all this with a sense of satisfaction and pressed the final command into the control panel to send his revenge on its way.

The rocket engine fired, flames from the propellant bounced off the shielding causing huge amounts of thrust, which was turned into kinetic energy, and the rocket lifted off, heading straight up into the night sky. Lassiter walked out onto the launch area and looked up to watch the flaming tail fly up in a straight line high into the sky before finally arcing over to change vector on its final trajectory.

"Nothing can stop me now," he said as he drew his pistol and waited for the intruders to show.

"What the fuck was that?" Sanchez said when they heard the rumble of the wall opening to allow the launcher to slide free from the basement.

"He's getting ready to launch," Duncan said and ran for the basement door. It was in the kitchen, and they were close by. He reached for the door controls.

Another sound filled the area, the sound of the rocket taking off.

"We're too late," Sanchez said. "He's already launched."

There had to be a way to stop this. Duncan knew now more than ever he had to get down into that cellar and abort that rocket, or everyone on this planet would die.

Pulling open the door, he stepped onto the first step leading down.

Bullets struck the doorframe close to his face. Splinters flew from the impacts, showering his face with wood chips. Ducking back into the kitchen, he fired around the door frame down at where he thought his shooter was. He didn't have time for this. He had to get down there, but as long as Lassiter had that gun, he held the advantage.

Bullets fired back at him, striking the frame once more. He counted the shots being fired and waited for them to stop.

His clip was empty. Now was his time to move.

Rushing onto the stairs, he held his SAP10 in front of him. He had every intention of killing Lassiter on sight for what he'd done.

Racing down the stairs, he came halfway down when something struck him across his legs. He went tumbling head-first down the rest of the stairs, rolling onto his back as he tried to control the fall.

When he looked up, Lassiter was standing over him, holding a long rod of some description. Covering up, he blocked the blows that his attacker rained down on him with the hard metal rod. Pain exploded across his arms where the blows landed, and in desperation, he lashed out with a leg, catching

Lassiter at the side of his knee, which crumpled his legs, dropping him to the floor as well.

Duncan rolled onto his knees and dropped onto Lassiter, pinning him to the ground as he hit him several times with his elbow to his head. Lassiter was also desperate and was fighting like a fury. He had the insane strength of someone twice his size. He easily pushed Duncan from him, and they both got to their feet, staring at each other. Duncan saw the feral look in Lassiter's eyes and knew he was totally insane.

"You can't stop it, you know," he taunted.

"But that means you die as well," Duncan said.

"But I'll die knowing I won. I got my revenge on those who took everything from me," Lassiter said, his eyes wide with insanity.

"It won't do you any good, though, if you're dead, will it?" Duncan said.

"It's a small price to pay," Lassiter said, and Duncan knew there was no point in trying to reason with him. He was beyond that now and into the realms of madness where winning was everything to him despite losing his own life in it all.

He had to act, so he rushed him, tackling him around the waist and slamming him into the wall. He slammed an elbow into the side of his head.

"How do I abort the rocket?" he shouted at him. He was beginning to lose his own control as he fought to save all those lives on this world.

"You can't," Lassiter replied, blood dripping through his shattered mouth. Then he held up the control module in his hand, "not without this," he added.

Duncan tore his eyes from his face to the module, giving Lassiter time to move. He brought up his knee, hitting Duncan squarely in the groin. Pain exploded in his nether regions, dropping him to the floor. Waves of nausea washed over him as stars danced before his eyes. Clamping his teeth together, he tried to control the pain and get back into the fight, but as anyone who's ever been kicked in the genitals knows, it's not that easy. It is one area on a man guaranteed to end any ideas of a fight, as all you want to do is curl up and wait for the pain to go away. The discomfort lasts for ages after the pain finally subsides and remains tender long after the shock of being hit.

Duncan knew all this. It wasn't the first time he'd had a blow land there, but like all the other times, this was just as painful, just as debilitating.

Through his pain-filled gaze, he saw Lassiter reach the opening in the wall where the rocket launcher had exited. Bullets struck the wall at the side, sending chips into his eyes as he looked back at Duncan to gloat.

Sanchez had arrived, seen what had happened, and fired at Lassiter.

"Get after him," croaked Duncan from his foetal position on the floor. His voice sounded like his throat was coated in broken glass.

Sanchez ran down the remaining stairs and gave chase, with Duncan waving her on.

As she disappeared through the opening, he tried to get to his feet. The pain was enormous, so he concentrated all his remaining energy on locking it away. He had to continue; he had to stop Lassiter and abort the rocket. A moment's calm was all he needed to channel his thoughts, get them under control, and lock off his emotions. He needed to be the perfect killing machine, totally without remorse, if he wanted to prevent this disaster from happening. He had to do what needed to be done, whatever the cost.

Opening his eyes, he felt a calm wash over him like a warm shower soothing away all his doubt and pain.

He was ready at last.

Chapter 38

A cry from outside the basement alerted him to Sanchez's plight. As he exited the small room, he saw his partner lying on the ground, Lassiter standing over her holding her SAP10 on her about to fire.

Acting quickly, he leaped at Lassiter, tackling him around the waist. His shoulder hit Lassiter squarely in his stomach as his hand reached for the hand holding the pistol, pushing it upwards as he fired. The bullet went high into the air, missing the target entirely.

Duncan landed on top of Lassiter as they rolled on the floor. He slapped the pistol free from his hand before getting kicked off him. The weapon went skittering across the floor to land several feet away, close to the base of the launcher.

Both men got to their feet, eyeing each other.

"Give me that module, Lassiter, I have to end this now," Duncan shouted at his enemy.

"Why end it? They all deserve to die," Lassiter replied, his eyes wide in fervour.

"You're insane; you realise that, don't you?" Duncan said.

"Am I?"

At that moment, Duncan knew he was a lost cause. He charged him once more, but before he could get within reach of him, Lassiter threw the module down on the floor as hard as he could. The small device shattered into tiny fragments, which Lassiter stomped into even smaller pieces underfoot. He smiled at Duncan as his foot ground the device into dust, ensuring that it could never be used again.

"You madman, you've just condemned us all to death," he shouted at the grinning lunatic.

"I know. Wonderful, isn't it," Lassiter said, laughing wildly.

Duncan picked up the fallen SAP10 and fired a single shot. The bullet slammed into the forehead of the madman, silencing his wild laughter once and for all.

"Shit, Duncan, what're we gonna do now?" Sanchez shouted when she realised their last chance to abort the rocket had just died with Lassiter.

"You're going to leave; I'm going to destroy that rocket," Duncan replied.

Hastily running scenarios through his mind and dismissing the ones he knew wouldn't work, he ran for the edge of the cliff where the villa sat.

"Ship, I need you now," he shouted and was relieved to hear a familiar voice in his ear, "On my way, Commander."

His ship didn't take long to rise from below the cliff face. The rear ramp dropped open, and as she hovered a few feet from the cliff edge, Duncan ran and leaped across the distance, landing on the edge of the ramp. Pulling himself into the hold, he scrambled to his feet.

"Get after that rocket," he said as he ran forward through the hold towards the pilot's section.

The ship fired the main burner, boosting her speed close to maximum. Inertia dampeners prevented him from being turned to mush against the hull as the speed increased to Mach ten.

When he reached the pilot's chair, straps wrapped around him when he sat down.

"Where's the rocket?" he asked. An image of the rocket in flight flashed the Heads Up Display. It was several thousand klicks in front in horizontal flight.

"Increase speed; we need to get within firing range," he ordered.

"Will be within firing range in three minutes thirty-three seconds, Commander," the ship replied.

"Charge the weapons and activate the targeting sensors," Duncan said.

"Copy that, Commander," the AI replied.

The Heads Up Display changed to show the targeting sensors' crosshairs following the image of the rocket. The crosshairs glowed red at the moment, indicating that they were still out of range.

The rocket was flying in a straight line as it closed in on the target it was programmed to hit, making it easier to track and chase.

Duncan was aware of the clock ticking down. They were still over a full minute from catching up when the rocket began its downward arc.

"How close to the target?" Duncan asked.

"I have extrapolated all the data from its trajectory and amount of fuel available, and given what we know about Lassiter and his recent activities…"

"Short version, Ship," Duncan said, interrupting the AI.

"The rocket has begun the final approach and will reach the target in forty-five seconds, Commander."

"We don't have enough time to wait for targeting sensors to get a lock on, fire now," Duncan said.

"The chances of me hitting the target are eleven percent, Commander."

"Take your best shot, Ship. I trust you," Duncan said.

"I am uncomfortable with this, Commander," the AI replied.

"Ship, take the shot now," Duncan demanded.

The forward pulse cannons fired, strafing the sky with high calibre rounds. The shells traced a path across the night sky as friction lit them up into virtual starbursts.

The first salvo missed by mere inches, passing harmlessly over the rocket as it arced down toward the city below.

"Fire again; give it everything we have," Duncan said.

The pulse cannons fired again, this time clipping one of the fins and sending it spinning off target.

Duncan took over control of the targeting and firing systems and fired a missile at the rocket. He knew that just because it had been knocked off target, it still had the potential to destroy all life on the planet.

His eyes were glued to the HUD as he watched the missile fly off, aimed at the rocket. His eager anticipation was kept in check by a strict control of his emotions. He was still aware of his breathing increasing slightly as he followed the missile until it got close and held his breath as he waited for the result he sorely needed.

The explosion lit up the night sky as the missile hit the rocket. A fireball spread outwards, incinerating the virus inside the warhead.

The danger was finally at an end.

Duncan observed the explosion holding his breath until he saw the results. When the fireball dissipated, there was nothing left of either the missile or the rocket, and he finally let out his breath.

"All traces of the Omega Five virus have vanished, Commander," the AI said.

"Thank you, Ship. Let's head back to base," Duncan replied as he relinquished the controls and sat back in the chair, finally able to relax.

Chapter 39

Duncan returned to cheers and applause from his colleagues in SecOps, which baffled him. Being in mission mode still, the emotions of others were something of a mystery and something he could never quite grasp. He was becoming more separated emotionally from them each day, and the thought that someday he might never find a way to be normal again often invaded his mind.

Keeping his eyes averted from them as he walked through the corridors to C's office, he actually felt confused by the praise. After all, he was just doing his job.

The thought of all those lives under threat had been at the forefront of his mind. It was his prime motivation for trying so hard to prevent it from happening, but facing the gratitude of some of the people his actions had saved was something he was not used to.

"Come in, Duncan," Chambers said as he entered the office. "Extremely well done out there. It was touch and go for a moment there, and everyone on this planet owes their lives to you, even if the majority of them had no idea what was happening," he added.

Duncan stood in front of the desk saying nothing, his eyes averted from the man seated at the desk. He stood at attention, waiting, unsure what to say or how to process it all. The enormity of what he'd done had never occurred to him. It was simply the right thing to do.

"I know how difficult this must be for you, Duncan, all this gratitude from your colleagues, but what you have to understand is what you did for them was a really big thing. You literally saved their lives, all of them, mine included. So forgive me for saying this, but you'll just have to put up with it for a while at least."

"Understood, sir," Duncan replied uncomfortably.

"Okay, back to work then. Lassiter is dead, and the threat of this Assembly for Criminal Enterprise died with him," Chambers said.

"Why would you say that, sir?" Duncan asked.

"Because you killed him, didn't you?"

"I meant, why would you assume Lassiter was the head of this organisation?"

Chambers sat back in his chair. This was something that had never occurred to him. They had all assumed Lassiter was the leader of this group. The thought that he was simply another pawn had never even entered into the equation.

"I hope you have something to back up that theory because everyone over in the Council headquarters is doing cartwheels of joy at the threat being over. What have you got to supplement your theory?"

"Lassiter was unstable, completely unravelling at the end, so I seriously doubt someone like that could control an organisation that has eluded detection for as long as I think this group has. It would take meticulous planning, and a mind that would come apart so easily at the first sign of difficulty just would not be capable of pulling that off. That's just my opinion, though, sir."

"You have a point, though. What do you suggest? Because with Lassiter dead, we have no leads left."

"Solvig. We have him, sir. He could lead us to whoever is behind all this."

"Okay, if what you say is true, then he won't suspect anything. He'll presume that we believe the threat is over, like everyone else, so we need to act fast. We'll go over there now and catch him off guard."

Duncan gave a nod of agreement. All his earlier pain and fatigue were soon forgotten as the game was still in play. Calling on reserves of strength and stamina, he was ready to carry on and see this through to the end.

The Council meeting was still underway when Duncan and Director Chambers arrived.

Solvig was at the side of James Marshall, as always, nodding along and agreeing with everything he said like the lap dog he was. His demeanour changed instantly when the two newcomers entered the room.

President Parris looked at them and said, "Well, gentlemen, nice of you to drop in unannounced. What is the meaning of your visit?"

Solvig had sat up straighter in his chair. It was an involuntary reaction to seeing the both of them enter.

C said, "I've come to speak with Thomas Solvig, sir. I have reason to believe he can give us the information we need to put an end to this situation."

"I thought it had been put to an end?" Parris said.

"That is what we are here to find out, sir."

"This is outrageous," erupted Marshall, springing to his feet.

"With respect, sir. This has nothing to do with you," C replied.

"Thomas Solvig has been a valuable asset to this government. If you are insinuating that he had something to do with anything illegal, then you have got it wrong, I assure you," Marshall continued.

"And if you're wrong, do you really want to be associated with him?" C pushed.

This made Marshall think. His priority had always been his self-preservation. He would never allow anything to stand in the way of that. The mere thought that he would be spoken of in the same breath as a criminal was anathema to him.

He moved in his seat, visibly distancing himself from Solvig, leaning away from him.

"You're conspicuously quiet in all of this, Mister Solvig. Do you have anything to add to any of this?" President Parris asked.

"Only to agree with what Defence Director Marshall said. This is preposterous. That you think it even faintly possible I could be caught up with this terrorist attack is, quite frankly, ludicrous," Solvig said.

"No one mentioned anything about the terrorist attacks. In fact, we never said exactly what we are here for," C said.

"I think you'd better go with them, Thomas, to sort this out," President Parris said, to which Solvig reluctantly got to his feet to comply.

Duncan saw his expression as he stood up, like that of a trapped animal caught in the sights of a predator. It was thinly veiled desperation, so he kept watching in case Solvig did something desperate people do in these situations—try to escape.

As Solvig left the table, Duncan saw the look on Marshall's face as he sat upright once more. His lips pressed together for just a second in anger, then relaxed. It was almost as if he didn't want anyone seeing his mask slip, or it could just be that he was angry at Solvig for duping him. Now he had to put on a confident face once more to try and ride out the storm that eventually would follow.

"Come with us, please, Mister Solvig, and answer some questions we have. If you're lucky and answer truthfully, then you can be back in time for breakfast," C said as Solvig joined them.

"With that, gentlemen and ladies, I think we can finally call it a night. Business as usual tomorrow, everyone. Go home and get some sleep," Parris said to the table as C, Duncan, and Solvig left the room.

Chapter 40

The transport was still on the landing pad close to the Council headquarters, with the pilot and guard waiting for their return.

Duncan followed C and Solvig into the shuttle, keeping an eye on their six to ensure they weren't being followed. As the door closed behind them, the guard took the co-pilot's chair up front while the three passengers got comfortable behind them in the sealed-off passenger section.

"Okay, Thomas, we know you work for this group calling themselves the Assembly for Criminal Enterprise, so why don't you tell me all you know about them, starting with the name of the person in charge?" C said. Sitting directly opposite Solvig, he looked into the man's eyes as he spoke. What he saw disturbed him. Instinctively he knew there wasn't going to be an awful lot they could learn from him, but they had to try.

Duncan was sitting next to Solvig, facing C, and listening to him question their prisoner.

"I don't know what you're talking about," Solvig said, his voice a little shaky.

Duncan hit him in the side of his head with an elbow strike, smashing his head against the hull he was next to.

"We don't have time for this bullshit. Tell us what we want to know, or this ride will get extremely painful for you," he said, his voice calm and steady. He spoke in a conversational tone that was unnerving. There were no histrionics from him, no false bravado or fake anger, just cold hard facts delivered dispassionately. Solvig knew instantly that Duncan meant every word he said.

"We all wore masks and voice disruptors so everyone's identity could be kept secret," Solvig replied, breaking down a little as he allowed his fear to show through his façade of bravery. He rubbed the side of his face where he'd been hit, looking sideways at Duncan but also trying to keep looking at the man opposite.

"Where did you meet?" C asked.

"We all arrived on Tau Ceti III but were transported to the meeting place inside a transporter that had no windows. We never saw where we were or how we got there. It was the same for the return journey. They took exceptional precautions to ensure no one knew where the meeting took place," Solvig replied.

"What about your tracker? Did they disable it or block it somehow?" Duncan asked. Solvig turned in his seat to look at him. Leaning away from him, he said, "I have no idea."

Duncan looked at C. "If they didn't disable or block it, then we can use it to track where he went, sir," he said.

"As soon as we reach HQ, I'll get the tech guys right on to it," C replied.

They had been in the air for less than ten minutes when the pilot issued a warning.

"We have a tango on our tail, guys. I suggest you strap yourselves in. This could get a little bumpy," he said.

Solvig's eyes went wide in terror.

Harnesses wrapped around them, moulding them to the seats. Now firmly in place, there was nowhere for them to go.

The shuttle was not built for dog fighting in the air, so when the pilot threw the craft into a series of tight twists and turns, the passengers were glad they were wearing harnesses.

The hull was peppered with shells from the attacking craft. Holes appeared where the bullets penetrated as they passed through.

"We're gonna die," screamed Solvig as he clenched the armrests so tight his knuckles went white.

"Who are these people?" C asked.

"You have to ask that, sir?" Duncan said through clenched teeth as he was being thrown around in his chair like the others. "I'd like to know how they knew where we were," he added.

"Good point. If we survive this, it's something we definitely should look into.

The shuttle was rocked again by cannon fire from the attacking craft and went into a nosedive.

Duncan suspected the worst and slammed a hand against the quick-release button in the centre of the harness, freeing himself. Holding on tight, he got out of his seat and ran forward; the downward angle of the shuttle threw him forward. He slammed into the doors to the pilot's cabin and operated the release, opening the door.

Inside, the windows had been shattered, and fragments of glass littered the bodies being pressed into the seats as they plummeted towards the ground. Both the pilot and guard were dead from multiple gunshot wounds. Blood was painted across the instruments, which, thankfully, looked unharmed.

He released the pilot from his seat, allowing him to fall forward, then took his seat. Grabbing the control stick, he pulled back, trying to drag the nose level, then up to prevent it from crashing.

Straining his arms to their absolute limits, he pulled on the controls. Through the shattered windows, he saw the ground coming up at an alarming speed and doubted he would have time to rectify their nose dive in time.

Finally, his arms shaking at the effort, the control stick began to react and come towards him. The nose, ever so slowly, began to rise up. Hope rose for just an instant inside him, blooming like a flower opening its petals to the morning sun, but it was not enough.

They were in the city, and their descent had taken them down into one of the streets. Buildings rose up on either side of them like the teeth of a gigantic mouth about to swallow them whole. Duncan saw people down on the streets running for their lives as they saw death aiming straight for them, scattering like ants before a massive foot about to step on them.

"Hang on, we're going in," he shouted when he was certain a crash was inevitable.

The ground came rushing towards him, and he gave the stick one last pull to try and raise the nose into a horizontal position before they crashed.

There was nothing left to do but hope they survived what came next as they hit the ground and everything turned to chaos.

Chapter 41

Duncan had tried to put the shuttle down in as quiet a street as possible.

When they hit the ground, the shuttle careened across the street, smashing into vehicles on the street that hadn't moved out of the way in time.

People ran for cover as the craft skidded down the street, smashing through vehicles and knocking them out of its path. Sparks flew out behind, tracing its path until they ignited and soon became a flaming tail.

Duncan had covered himself with his arms as they hit the ground, but when he was certain they had landed on their belly instead of going nose-first into the ground, he regained hold of the stick, trying to steer it somehow. The brakes weren't functioning as the landing gear failed to operate, so he had to hope for the best.

Finally, friction caused them to slow down. A glance in the rear told him of another danger, one just as bad as the crash.

Flames were spreading from the friction outside the shuttle to the rear quarters of the craft.

He jumped out of his seat and ran into the passenger section.

"We have to get out of here now. This shuttle is going to blow," he told the other two.

C was already aware of the fire as he was facing the rear and saw the flames starting to take hold and grow in intensity.

Duncan helped the two men from their seats and assisted in guiding them to the hatch in the side of the hull. As he opened the hatch, it slid into a recess in the hull, and wind from their path rushed inside.

"Are you mad? You want us to jump?" shouted Solvig over the sound of screeching metal and fire from outside.

Duncan didn't answer. He simply grabbed the man and hurled him through the opening.

"After you, sir," he said to his boss, who braced himself and then launched himself from the hatch.

Duncan gave one final look down the craft to see the flames closing in on him. He could feel the heat from them as he threw himself through the hatch into the street beyond.

He hit the ground hard and was sent rolling down the street, bouncing off the hard pavement until he came to a stop. His body ached from what seemed like a million places, and he was breathing hard. He looked at the shuttle, which was by then a blazing wreck. It came to a stop by slamming into the front of a building and then exploded as the power cells burst caused by the fire. The fireball blew outwards and crawled up the front of the building before it dissipated. The shockwave from the blast blew out the windows of several buildings on the same side as well as opposite it, scattering shards of glass over everything.

Duncan held his hands over his head as he flattened into the ground to protect himself from the blast. Flaming pieces of debris reached him even that far away, and he waited for it to extinguish itself before getting up and patting down his clothing which was already smouldering.

He ran back to where the other two were to check on them, and when he reached them, he saw what had assaulted them. An attack helicopter was racing toward them, aiming its front cannons at them.

"Come on, you two, we're not out of the woods just yet," he said, grabbing them and racing into the nearest building.

"We need to get to the roof. We might be able to fend them off from there while you call in backup," Duncan said, dragging the two men inside with him. Through the door, a wide-open space spread before them. He hadn't noticed which building he'd chosen, just that it was available. It was a huge mall with the ground floor stretching out for hundreds of feet before them. Shops on either side lined the sides of this floor with a grand twin escalator taking centre stage.

"This way," Duncan said as he headed for the escalator to take them up to the next floor.

Shoppers all around them were either running deeper into the mall or rushing towards the exit to see what the commotion was outside. As the three of them hit the escalator, the chopper hovered lower outside the entrance, firing the forward cannon inside.

Shells tore up the shop fronts, sending shattered glass everywhere, covering everyone and the floor. Bodies were shredded by the gunfire, sending bloodied body parts spinning in every direction.

"Run!" Duncan shouted as he pushed the other two men in front of him up the moving staircase.

A squad of four men dropped to the ground from the chopper, all armed with assault rifles, and immediately headed towards the entrance of the mall. Pushing aside anyone who got in their way, they soon made it through the crowd and were inside.

They spotted the three men escaping up the escalator and opened fire.

Duncan kept his attention diverted between what was in front and behind them. When he saw the four hunters enter, he pushed the men off the escalator at the top just as they began shooting at them.

He was just in time as bullets struck the handrails less than three seconds after they disappeared off the escalator.

"Keep moving, there's four of them after us on foot," Duncan said as he urged them deeper inside the mall.

They forged ahead through the shoppers who were on this floor. Many were oblivious to the chaos about to visit them and were startled by the sudden arrival of these three men.

Duncan led them towards the rear of the floor, hoping to find an exit that would lead them to the roof. If they could get there, he could call his ship, and they'd have a way off as well as a way to fight back.

Running as fast as he could, he was keeping pace with C. Even though C was much older than him, Duncan was barely keeping in front of the older man.

The three of them jumped when they heard gunfire behind them.

Duncan turned his SAP10 out and returned fire. His first shot hit the leading gunman in the chest, knocking him back on his heels. The others scattered to the sides, looking for cover as they fired back.

The instant gunfire was heard, everyone on the floor became suddenly aware of what was happening and rushed to find sanctuary in the shops. The floor in between was quickly cleared of anyone except the four gunmen and the three men they were chasing.

Duncan saw what he was looking for up ahead. A door leading to the fire escape.

"Over there, go through that door," he urged, and C complied, dragging Solvig with him. Duncan covered them as they pushed through the door and then followed, firing off a few more shots to discourage the gunmen.

"We need to go up," Duncan said and started running up the stone stairs. They'd gone up two flights when he heard the door slam open below them.

The gunmen had followed them.

"Keep going," he urged the other two.

By the time they had run up another flight, Duncan's lungs were burning, and his legs were beginning to feel like lead weights, but still, he pushed on through the pain.

From below, the gunmen were racing up after them, occasionally firing up the middle, hoping a stray bullet would catch one or more of them. The shots echoed loudly in the narrow stairwell, bouncing off the walls, making it difficult to pinpoint where the sound originated.

Finally, they reached the top and burst through the door onto the roof. Slamming the door closed behind them, Duncan leaned his back against it, his lungs heaving from the exertion. Not having a second to spare, though, he called his ship.

"Ship, come to my location immediately. We are in need of evac now," he said breathlessly.

"Copy that, Commander. I have been monitoring your progress and am on my way. ETA thirty seconds," the AI responded.

"We might not have thirty seconds, Ship," Duncan said as he looked around the wide expanse of the roof for somewhere they could use for cover should the gunmen breach this door.

"Copy that, sir," the AI said.

"We're gonna die," Solvig bleated now that he'd got his breath back.

"Control yourself, man," C said, wanting to slap him, but thought better of it. He decided he would save his energy for better things. If they got out of this with their skin intact, Solvig would get his then.

The door they had come through was part of a structure that was built onto the roof, so there was space around the sides and back they could use. The rest of the roof was a wide-open space.

"Get behind there," Duncan said, pushing Solvig around the back of the door. "If they get through that door, I'll try to hold them off as long as I can. You get Solvig back to HQ and learn what you can from him," he added.

"This is not the time to play hero, son. We get out of this together," C said.

Duncan didn't have time to respond because the door exploded outward, putting an end to that conversation.

Chapter 42

Duncan pushed C behind him, shielding him from the blast. Door fragments and smoke, followed by a small, controlled fireball, spread out from the doorway across the rooftop. For a second or two, the doorway was concealed from view by the explosion, but when the smoke began to clear, he saw three figures coming through, rifles up and ready to fire.

Duncan fired a three-round salvo, hitting the first man in the head. His skull was shredded by the large calibre bullets from the SAP10, splashing the man next to him with blood and gore.

Duncan retreated behind the back of the door. The other two men ran out across the roof, spreading out to give Duncan more than one target. He saw what they were doing and targeted one and was about to fire when they started firing. Bullets whizzed past him, narrowly missing their mark. He had to retreat back behind the doorway structure or get hit. Bullets ricocheted off the Plascrete structure, sending chips flying into the air. Duncan covered up, unable to fire back.

It was just a matter of time before they homed in on him, and it would be all over.

He saw one of the shooters advancing, and he brought up his SAP10, but before he could fire, a hail of cannon fire struck the gunman. He danced like a puppet as the shots ripped through him, painting the rooftop with his blood. The salvo quickly ended, and the body lay on the floor, a tangled bloody mess, while the shooter came into view.

Duncan breathed a sigh of relief as he saw his ship fly over the roof as it went after the last gunman. More gunfire was heard, and he knew their relief had arrived literally in the nick of time.

The ship came into view once more as it came in to land, and the rear ramp dropped, allowing them to enter.

"I hope I was not too late, Commander," the AI said.

"You arrived just in time, Ship, and thank you," Duncan replied, "What about that attack chopper that dropped those men off?" he asked.

"How do you want to deal with it, sir?" the AI asked.

"Blow it the hell out of the sky," C said.

"You heard the boss," Duncan said.

"Copy that, sirs," the AI replied. As it lifted off from the roof, Duncan took the front seat. He watched the sensor screens and saw the chopper coming in from the rear quarter, aiming to attack. The AI controlled all the weapon systems and activated the missile pods. Two independent pods dropped from concealed holds in the hull and rotated around to face the rear while the targeting sensors locked onto the chopper. A warning beep signalled they had a hard target lock on the aircraft, which was duplicated on the sensor screen Duncan was watching. The crosshairs changed colour from red to green before the AI fired.

Two missiles streaked toward the chopper, which didn't have time to move out of the way. The twin explosions lit up the night sky as a fireball spread out across the rooftops.

Flaming debris rained down on the street below as the destroyed chopper fell from the air. The threat was over, for now.

"That takes care of that," he said. Turning to the others, he said, "Let's go. If I remember correctly, Mister Solvig, you have some questions to answer."

The flight back to headquarters was uneventful, and Solvig was escorted to an interrogation room while C informed the president of the attack on them after leaving him.

He was as worried by that development as C was. It meant there was someone inside that room who either informed them of Solvig being taken or that they had been under surveillance all the time. Either option was unbearable to contemplate for long. The implications were dire because it meant this group was not dead in the water like they'd hoped but was instead alive and well and willing to continue the fight.

When C returned to the interrogation room, Duncan was already sitting opposite Solvig, staring at him with his cold hard eyes.

As he sat down next to Duncan, he said, "Okay, Thomas, let's get started, shall we? Who is in charge of ACE?"

"I've already answered that. I have no idea," Solvig replied.

Duncan said, "On our way here, I had my ship run a scan on your tracker. We now know where on Tau Ceti III you visited. We're running searches for whoever else connected to you visited the same location at the same times as you."

Solvig looked at him in wonderment, "And?" he asked.

"Well, I know it will take some time to whittle down all the names, but eventually, we'll find the one or ones we want, and then this little group of yours will get torn apart," Duncan said in a calm tone.

"In the meantime, though, I am sending Duncan to the location on Tau Ceti III to see what's out there," C said.

Duncan rose to his feet, as did C, who said, "Make yourself comfortable, Solvig. You're going to be here for a while just yet."

Outside the room, C said, "You have the coordinates in your ship. Get over there and learn what you can about this group and, if possible, shut them down. Agent Sanchez will be acting as your backup, as usual. Good luck, Agent Pryde."

"Thank you, sir," Duncan said.

When he boarded his ship, he was taken aback slightly by the presence of Sanchez sitting in the pilot's chair.

"What're you doing here?" he asked.

"I'm fine, thanks. I had my own ride off that island, but nice of you to ask," she replied, which drew a confused look from Duncan.

"Why are you here?" he asked again, ignoring her comments.

"To help you. I thought that was obvious," she replied.

"C said you were my backup, but he never said anything about you coming along with me."

"He knew you'd complain or refuse or some such nonsense if he told you. Best not to tell you, but let you find out this way. Ship, take off, please, and transport us to Tau Ceti III," she said. She stood up and waved him to the chair with a smile. "I've restocked the weapons and added a few extras in case we need them. If where we're going is the headquarters of this group, then it's best we go in prepared for the worst, don't you think?" she said,

"Okay, you can come. Just don't get in my way."

"When are you going to accept that we make a good team?" she asked, annoyed at his attitude.

"I'm not a team player and never will be. I work best alone; that way, I don't have to worry about anyone else getting hurt, and I can concentrate on the job at hand."

She looked at him deeply, probably truly seeing him for the first time. "That must make you very lonely, Duncan. You don't have to live that way," she said.

"You make it sound like a choice. It's not. It's the way I am. I can't change it any easier than I can prevent the sun from rising. This is me, accept it or not, your choice," he said, sitting down.

Sanchez said nothing; she just bowed her head in defeat and then left the bridge.

Chapter 43

As Duncan and Sanchez took off, C waited in the Situation Room. He desperately wanted to go to sleep, but he had to see this through.

He had this nagging feeling that they were very close, but one slight slip, one misstep, would send them down the wrong path, and it could all start over again. He couldn't allow that to happen. He had to ensure this group was ended tonight.

"Any news on who else might be involved in this?" he asked.

Goodchild came over to him and said, "There is one name that cropped up, sir, someone who makes frequent visits to Tau Ceti III but was overlooked at first."

"Goodchild, why are you still here?" he asked.

"If you and Duncan are still working on this, sir, it felt wrong somehow not to be here doing everything I could to help."

"I appreciate that. You have no idea how much."

"Thank you, sir."

"Now, who's name cropped up?"

"Defence Director James Marshall, sir. We overlooked him at first because he has a home there, so it's obvious he would visit from time to time. The thing is, sir, his visits coincide with those of Thomas Solvig."

C smiled, possibly for the first time in a day or two. "Well done, Goodchild. That's exceptional work. Do you have a location on him at the moment?"

"He left the Council Headquarters shortly after you and Duncan did, sir. He's on his way to Tau Ceti III."

"Get in touch with Duncan immediately. Inform them of our findings. If we're lucky, this could all end tonight."

"Copy that, sir," she said and left him in the middle of the room to make the call.

Tau Ceti III

Duncan looked at the planet below once they cleared the hyperspace window. He saw a blue orb floating in the endless darkness of space broken only by the spots of light coming from stars millions of light years away. Tau Ceti III was an Earth Class planet, one of the Goldilocks planets, neither too hot nor too cold, with just the right atmosphere, the same as Earth.

One of the first planets to be colonised, it now had a population of over three hundred million people and was growing every day. It had three major land masses and five oceans. The coordinates he'd been given for the suspected headquarters of ACE were near the coast of the largest land mass.

When he received the call from Goodchild about Marshall, it somehow made sense it would be him. He had quite cleverly appeared to be nothing more than a career politician, a rich kid who entered politics because the family expected it of him but had no real passion nor skill at it. To bolster this image, he seemed to rely heavily on his aide, Solvig, giving everyone the impression it was Solvig who was the real master and Marshall nothing more than a meat puppet.

To bolster this image, he seemed to rely heavily on his aide, Solvig, giving everyone the impression it was Solvig who was the real master and Marshall nothing more than a meat puppet.

It was a ruse, and now he knew it was just that. He could see it for how clever it was. No one suspected him of being capable of doing anything remotely as audacious as this, so he was left alone to pull the strings behind the scenes as he skillfully pulled the wool over everyone's eyes.

"Are you impressed by him?" Sanchez asked when she saw his expression and slight smile after bringing her up to speed.

"I have to admit, yes, I am, just a little, but only by the audacity of it all, nothing more than that. To pull this off under everyone's nose while misdirecting us all to someone else, you have to admit, it takes a certain kind of person with the balls to pull something like that off."

When he saw her open-mouthed disgust, he had to clarify, "It won't affect how I deal with him, though. I can admire his skill but still take him down. He threatened the lives of millions of people, and for that, he must be punished. It's not enough to just stop him now. We have to prevent him from ever being able to do anything like this again," he said.

"You don't think putting him behind bars in a penal colony is enough then?"

"We have to send a clear message here. One that says, if you fuck with us, we'll fuck with you just as hard, if not harder. If we lock him away, it sends a message to others like him that we are soft, weak. We don't have the balls to fight back. Sometimes you have to make the hard choices to get the result you need."

"Well, at least we agree on something then."

"Ship, take us down close to the coordinates we were given, please. Let's take a look at what we're dealing with here," Duncan said.

The orbiting controllers recognised the ship's authentication codes and allowed them to enter their space. She went down through the atmosphere and towards the largest land mass, Europa. The coastal area was populated by waterfront properties that backed onto the city beyond.

"The coordinates are that building directly ahead of us, Commander. It belongs to James Marshall," the AI said.

The building indicated was surrounded by a high wire fence, cordoning it off from the rest of the waterfront properties. It was a large three-story building with skylights on the roof to allow more sun into the top-floor rooms. Two large marble columns stood on either side of the front door, holding up a porch that sheltered the front from rain. Large windows on every floor gave them an abundance of natural light during the summer months.

"He's done well for himself," Sanchez commented on the opulence of his home.

"Let's take a closer look," Duncan said.

Inside the huge house, the alert had already been given, and preparations were underway to deal with the threat.

Marshall sat in his office, watching the proceedings on a series of monitors that lined one entire wall. Cameras were fitted around his property, providing a three-hundred-and-sixty-degree view around him. If anything moved close, he would see it.

He contacted his security staff through an earbud link.

"Okay, people, they're just two operatives, not a real threat, but let's not get cocky here. Take them out fast and efficiently. No slip-ups, okay?" he said to them.

From outside the property, hidden deep underground, rose gun turrets. Positioned near the fence on the edge of the grounds and operated remotely, these cannons began to track movement outside the perimeter fence. A rocket launcher rose from another concealed bunker underground and began doing the same.

Once his defences were in place and operating, Marshall felt the situation was under control.

In a hangar also hidden underground sat his private ship. Fitted with a Jump Drive and capable of sustaining him for almost a year, he could go anywhere and remain hidden until the dust settled. Then he would return to pick up the pieces with a new identity, as his present one was of no use to him anymore.

"Get ready, people. When they make their move, blow them out of the sky," he said.

Chapter 44

"Target those weapons and fire," Duncan said as he saw them rise up from underground.

If he had any doubts whoever lived at this house was involved in the recent activities, seeing those weapons appear wiped them from his mind.

Missiles were fired at the gun emplacements and, in quick order, blew them to bits leaving the area free for them to land.

Duncan was out of his seat, moving toward the hatch, when Sanchez appeared at his side.

"Where are you going?" he asked.

"With you, isn't that obvious?" she replied.

"No, you're staying here and keeping the ship in readiness if I need a fast exit. I don't need you slowing me down in there."

"Why would you think I'd slow you down?"

"Because I can't afford the time to think about your safety. I don't want you getting hurt out there."

"I'm as much an agent as you are. I'm going with you."

"I'm only going to say this once, and if you repeat it to anyone, I will deny it. I care about you, and I don't want to see you in danger. It will affect my performance, so please, stay here and be my backup. I'll call if I need you."

Sanchez was completely taken aback by that admission. It was completely out of character for the person who she thought she'd come to know. Then it made sense. All the times he'd told her that she got under his skin and annoyed her was a distraction. Those were the signs she had missed completely, and in her attempt to try and make him more human, she had succeeded in making him have feelings for her. Or had he had them already and kept them hidden, under control, just as he did with all his other emotions? She might never get to know because as she was pondering these thoughts, he'd taken advantage of her delay and left the ship, leaving her standing there, open-mouthed and a little shocked.

Duncan ran across the ground, passing the destroyed emplacements, feeling a little embarrassed at confessing his feelings for Sanchez, and he fought to keep that under control and concentrate on the job at hand. By the time he reached the building, he was his normal self, operating in mission mode.

He placed directed charges on the doors and stepped aside. Pressing the activator button detonated the explosives, and the doors were blown inwards in a controlled blast.

Duncan stepped into the doorway, his assault rifle up at his shoulder, ready to fire. Three figures appeared through the smoke, and he took aim and fired. Three shots rang out, and three bodies fell.

Progressing inside, Duncan looked for any sign of the owner of the house. Marshall was nowhere to be seen on the ground floor.

Touching his earbud, he said, "Ship, scan the building for life signs. Tell me where Marshall is."

"I have one signal moving down a staircase at the rear of the building to a basement.," the AI replied.

Duncan responded by running in the direction indicated. At the rear of this floor, he found a door. All the other doors led to rooms on the same floor, so he suspected he had found the one he needed. He pulled it open and headed down the staircase he found. The area below was lit, indicating someone was already down there.

He had found him.

Carefully, he progressed down the stairs looking for any signs of a threat from the owner. He was also aware there could be traps waiting for him, so he was on the alert for those, too.

The staircase had a bend in it, and as he approached it, he slowed, listening for any sound that would alert him to anyone being down there. Taking a step farther, he began to round the corner. Bullets hit the wall, forcing him back a step.

He primed a stun grenade, tossed it around the corner, and waited for the result, covering his ears and closing his eyes.

The small oval object bounced twice and then detonated. A flash of intense white light burst outward as a deafening blast of noise filled the small room, bouncing around and reverberating off the walls. Anyone caught in that would be incapacitated for minutes.

Duncan waited for a second or two while he regained his own senses, then went around the corner, his rifle aimed at the man standing in the centre of the room.

Marshall was wearing a sensory protection helmet that covered his eyes, ears, and mouth. The visor was up when Duncan entered this section of the basement, and he could see his eyes.

He also saw a pistol aimed right at him.

"I wouldn't do that if I were you," Marshall said, with all traces of his former character gone to be replaced by this calm, confident person standing in front of him.

"And why not?" Duncan asked.

"Because if you fire and kill me, you won't get the answers you so desperately need."

"So, what do we do now then?" Duncan asked, keeping his weapon aimed at Marshall.

"Why not put down our weapons and talk it out, like gentlemen," Marshall suggested.

"Okay," Duncan agreed and lowered his rifle, slowly bending at the waist to place it on the ground. He kept an eye on Marshall, who copied his movements until the very last second. When Duncan released his hold on the rifle, Marshall stood upright again, still holding his pistol.

"You are too trusting, something I never expected of you," he said.

Duncan's hand thrust out as he tossed his knife underhanded at Marshall. The blade struck the pistol, sending it spinning from his hand.

Marshall eyed him with a mixture of shock and anger.

"Who said I trusted you?" Duncan asked.

Marshall then ran at him, and the two men collided. Marshall pushed Duncan into the staircase, slamming his back against the stone steps.

Pain lanced across the agent's lower back, and he grimaced through it, gritting his teeth against the pain.

He brought his right elbow across Marshall's two arms to strike him across the side of his face. The blow rocked Marshall, snapping his head around. Blood ran from the cut on his cheek as he was sent back a step or two.

Duncan lashed out with a front kick to the stomach, sending Marshall back a few more steps grunting in pain from the blow.

Duncan came at him, but Marshall showed more skill at close-quarter combat than expected. He sidestepped his attack and brought up his left knee into Duncan's stomach. The blow caught him off guard and doubled him at the waist. A blow to the back of his head dropped him to the floor.

He was about to move when a kick to his head momentarily robbed him of his senses. He lay there, unable to move, stars dancing in front of his eyes as his head spun. All his recent exertions were beginning to catch up with him, and he was tired to the point of total exhaustion.

He was vaguely aware of Marshall moving around him doing something, of which he was not sure, but he knew he had to get up or face the chance of dying where he lay.

Fighting through his fatigue, he got to his feet, and Marshall turned from a console to look at him.

"It's all over, Agent Whoever-You-Are. You lost," he said.

Desperately trying to regain some strength, Duncan leaned against a nearby desk and asked, "What do you mean it's over?"

"I've just programmed a self-destruct signal to all the top agents working with me. All the members of my high council will soon be dead. They all had implants to show their loyalty. What they didn't know was the implant contained a miniature explosive with just enough power to blow their heads off. All that needs to be done now is to destroy everything here and leave for my new life away from all this. I'll wait a year or two for the dust to settle, then pick up where I left off. The infrastructure for my organisation will still be in place, and the rank and file will just be waiting for my next message, so it'll be easy."

"You've got it all planned out then," Duncan said, feeling some semblance of normality returning.

"From the very beginning. You see, there was always a chance that something like this would happen, so I made plans, and here we are."

"What if I stop you from leaving, stop your plans altogether?" Duncan asked.

With a wide grin, Marshall replied, "Well, you haven't done so well in that department so far, have you?"

"Oh, I'm just getting started," Duncan said.

Marshall reached behind him and activated something hidden from them both. A voice issued a warning, "Self-destruct in five minutes," it said.

The two men locked eyes across the room. The endgame had begun.

Chapter 45

Marshall made a dash for another door, hoping to leave Duncan behind him. He was not so successful.

Duncan slammed into him as he went through the door, sending them sprawling to the floor. They were in the underground hangar where Marshall stored his escape craft. It was a small yacht, and by the look of it, it was ready to launch.

Duncan hit Marshall several times in the head with elbow strikes, but in Duncan's weakened state, the blows weren't as effective as he'd like. Marshall rolled his attacker from him and regained his feet. He was no longer concerned with continuing the fight. He was more concerned about getting away before the self-destruct destroyed this entire area, his house, and everything around it.

Once he freed himself from Duncan's clutches, he raced for his yacht. Duncan was on his feet and ran after him, catching him at the hatch of the vessel. He grabbed a handful of Marshall's hair at the back of his head and slammed his face against the hull.

Blood smeared across the hull from Marshall's broken nose, and he back-elbowed Duncan away from him.

Not giving up, Duncan kicked him as hard as he could in his groin. Marshall's face contorted as pain exploded from his groin to every inch of his body. He clutched at his genitals as his knees bent, and he collapsed onto the floor in the foetal position.

"Tell me how to stop the self-destruct," he shouted at Marshall. There was a pause as the man on the ground was unable to do anything, not even speak. Finally, after Duncan shouted his question again at him, he said, "You can't. I added a failsafe into the programme so that once it started, there was no way to stop or abort it. This place will blow in less than two minutes."

"Are you saying there's nothing we can do?" Duncan asked, not giving up hope just yet.

"You could grab both ankles, put your head between your knees and kiss your ass goodbye."

"Jokes at a time like this?"

Marshall didn't answer; he just shrugged, then lashed out with his right leg, sweeping Duncan off his feet. He was up and running for the yacht as Duncan hit the ground.

Duncan took out his SAP10 and fired. His three shots hit Marshall in his back, stopping him instantly just as he reached the hatch.

Getting to his feet, he was so tired that all he wanted to do was lie down to sleep. Seeing Marshall dead before him, he knew that ACE was dead too. He'd as much as told him that all the high council members would soon be deceased; he was just sorry he'd not be around to see who they were. He knew he didn't have either the time or energy to get away in time, but he took solace in the fact that his mission had succeeded. So, looking at it from that perspective, maybe it was a good day to die.

"Duncan, give me a sit-rep. What's happening in there?" Sanchez said.

Duncan's voice sounded like that of a man who had given his all when he spoke. He said, "Sanchez, get clear now. Don't argue, just do it."

She reacted fast, "Ship, get us clear now," she said.

The engines fired, and as soon as they were off the ground, the ship moved away, boosting speed to put distance between them and the house.

The explosion came from deep below, lifting through all the floors, blowing walls off, and throwing the shattered roof high into the air, carried by a gigantic fireball.

"Oh my God, Duncan, what did you do?" she said as she watched the destruction in the rear viewer.

"He did nothing, Agent Sanchez; the house was set to self-destruct by Marshall. All Agent Pryde did was warn you so you could survive," the AI replied.

As soon as Duncan had warned Sanchez, he moved to the edge of the launch pad, which overlooked the sea beyond.

They were perched on a cliff edge high above the sea with cliffs and a sheer drop of around a hundred feet. He was looking down at the dark waters when the night around him lit up like a star bursting around him, and he knew what had happened.

The blast took him off his feet and hurled him over the cliffs to fall that seemingly impossible distance to the water below. When he hit the water, the bone-crushing impact took what was left of his senses, and he sank deep into the depths.

Chapter 46

The atmosphere in C's office the following day was sombre. Rescue parties had searched throughout the night and into the early morning with no result.

Duncan Pryde's body had not been found.

C was angry, "What were you thinking allowing him to go in there alone? You went against all protocols, and your actions cost an agent his life. Not just a good agent, but a good man and my friend," he raged. He paced across the width of his office behind his desk, unable to sit. He felt he had to do something, but there was nothing he could do, which only made him feel worse.

Sanchez stood in front of the desk; her head bowed as tears ran down her face, not because of the bollocking she'd just had but from her grief at losing Duncan. She had come to regard him as a friend, as well, despite his constant ignoring of her. In the end, she knew he cared for her, too. And now that was gone.

"I'm sorry, sir, you'll have my resignation as soon as this meeting is over," she said, her voice breaking with emotion.

"That won't be necessary, Agent Sanchez. I've no doubt that Duncan added to his own demise more than you have admitted. I know how that man operated, his damn lone wolf attitude. I told him it would get him killed. His only reply was, 'Better me than someone else, sir.' He was insufferable but a damn good agent and, like I said, my friend."

"What are we going to do, sir?" she asked.

"We carry on like normal. I read your first report about the incident on Tau Ceti III. According to your statement, you overheard a conversation between Duncan and Marshall where the latter said he'd sent a signal to the implant of every high council member of his organisation."

"Is that even possible, sir?"

"Oh, very possible. In fact, we've had reports of prominent citizens dropping dead from catastrophic injuries to their head arriving all morning."

"Anyone we know, sir?"

"Indeed, many corporate figures, even some from the government and the military, have suffered head trauma. It seems what you overheard may have been right. Marshall was clearing the deck so he could return one day to start afresh."

"What about Duncan, sir, will there be a funeral without a body?"

"We'll hold a service for him, send him off with full honours, but that's all we can do without a body."

"Have you informed his family?"

"He doesn't have any. His parents both died, and he has no siblings. I think we were his family."

"That is sad, don't you think, sir?"

"Very, but that's the kind of man he was. He was unique, but his very uniqueness brought with it setbacks of its own, one of which forced him to isolate himself from any personal connections. He lived for his work simply because I fear it was all he had."

"I think you're right, sir."

"How are you feeling? If you need some time off, take as long as you need. With this present operation coming to a close, things around here should be a lot quieter for the time being. So why don't you take some time off once you've surrendered your full report."

"Thanks, sir. I think I will. There are a few things I need to sort out before I return to work."

"Well, take as long as you need. If things get busy, I'll contact you. Until then, go get some rest."

Sanchez nodded and left the room.

Epilogue

After the service, C, Agent Sanchez, and Goodchild congregated in a bar near the HQ.

It had gone off without a hitch, organised by the redoubtable Goodchild, and was attended by a few members of SecOps and the three closest to him who later went off to a private service of their own.

The room they booked was small and convenient to their needs because they didn't intend to spend too long there. A few stories were told about their experiences with Duncan, but not too many as they soon realised that none of them had spent any considerable time with the man. Not to get to know him properly, at least, so they did what they could.

They remembered the man, gave toasts to him, and hoped that he was at peace wherever he was.

The end.

About the Author

Jan Domagala was born in Staffordshire, England to a working class family where at school he discovered the joys of reading. Jan was a big fan of sci-fi books but would read almost anything he could get his hands on. His mother took him to join the local library as soon as he could read and from that day on, if it had words on it, he'd read it.

In the early 70's there wasn't much choice for employment where Jan lived so he ended up in an apprenticeship in screen printing for the ceramic industry. In the early years of his apprenticeship he had the pleasure of a trip on the schooner Captain Scott, a training ship as part of the crew. They sailed around Scotland and even up as far as Stornoway in the Outer Hebrides.

Jan is still in the same trade after a forty year career, but his passion is and has always been writing. After several abortive attempts, he started the Col Sec series, which is an action-adventure series set in the twenty fifth century.

Jan is currently working on the next book in the series.

Join Jan by subscribing today!

http://eepurl.com/dLM3gk

Follow me on BookBub! https://www.bookbub.com/authors/jan-domagala

And on Facebook: https://www.facebook.com/ColSecSeries

Also by Jan Domagala

The Col Sec Series

Ronin

Omega

Discovery

BHASHANI, THE MOULANA
BHASHANI, THE COMRADE

DEWAN AREFIN